"ALL I WANT TO DO IS SURF"

VIA FRANCO
&
ART DURAND

THE BOND BETWEEN SURFERS is an authentic surf story of two childhood friends. Her ambition is to become world champion and he is trying to find the meaning of life through surfing. Follow a crew of surfers and immerse yourself into their world.

THE SURFING WORLD

THE BOND BETWEEN SURFERS

By

Mark Rebscher

Graphics By

Mark Rebscher

Inquiries at www.tbbsurf.com

DEDICATION

TO ALL THE SURFERS IN THE WORLD

ACKLOWDGEMENTS

John Marcucci

Debbie Boisvert

My Wife Monica

CONTENTS

PREFACE

I know this is an unconventional approach to making a movie, but hey…

Surfers are Masters of the Unconventional.

What does it mean to be a surfer? It can be answered 25 million ways, by 25 million surfers. This story is my version of what it means to be a surfer. I hope you enjoy the book and one day the film.

Only surfers understand surfers. That's why in order to make an authentic film, I would have to take it to the surfers of the world. I have converted the Screenplay Version of the story into a Book Version to build awareness and raise money to make it into a feature length film. If you believe in the story, I'm asking each and every one of the 25 million surfers to help me make this movie a reality. We can create a grass roots film. You've heard the saying, "Power to The People". My saying is…

POWER TO THE SURFERS!

This is your movie! A feature length film about surfers, made by surfers, financed by surfers. Be a part of surf history.

HOW CAN YOU CONTRIBUTE?

1. Spread the Word to All Surfers and Friends of Surfers

2. Make It Go Viral!

3. Buy the Book (Amazon)

4. Buy the E-Book (Amazon)

5. Buy the Audiobook (Amazon)

6. Listen to the Audio Episodes (Podcast)

7. Buy a T-shirt or Other Merch (Online)

8. Contribute to Patreon (Crowdfunding Site)

One day you will be sitting in the movie theater looking up at the big screen and you can proudly say, "I helped make this movie!"

For more information go to my website or scan the QR Code.

Thank You for believing in me and the vision,

Mark Rebscher

www.tbbsurf.com

POWER TO THE SURFERS!

ABOUT THE BOOK

Sticking with the unconventional, the book is written in screenplay format. A screenplay is a how to manual of a film. The story is written in an entirely different format with scene descriptions, camera angles, acting instructions, and dialogue lines. This is the actual script that will be used to make "The Bond Between Surfers" into a feature length film. The screenplay is a window, your back stage pass, into how movies are written and made.

I bypassed the traditional approach of selling the screenplay to a film studio. I always felt like the studios would not understand the script, try to change the story, and water down its authenticity. In order to keep the true surfer vision alive, I would have to raise the money to get the film made myself. I had to think of ways to get the story in front of the public eye. That's when I had the idea of self-publishing the screenplay in book format and take it directly to surfers and friends of surfers.

I have also created an **audiobook** and **audio episodes** of the screenplay. I have put together a **podcast** showcasing these audio episodes. I taught myself Graphic Art in order to create thumbnails for each episode. The graphics totally blew my mind. I managed to create images of the story that were in my head! A visual interpretation of my written words! I felt like I needed to do more with these graphics than just use them as thumbnails for the podcast. That's when I came up with the idea of inserting them into the book. Screenplays have strict formatting rules. One of those rules are No Illustrations in the Screenplay. But hey! We are surfers! Have we ever followed the rules? You can go to my website www.tbbsurf.com or scan the QR Code for more information about the Audio Episode Podcasts and the Audiobook.

A final note, I may not be the greatest writer or graphic artist in the world, but just like taking off on a big wave; I dropped in, never hesitated, and charged it! Hopefully, I will ride the wave of making a movie with glory

and grace. If not, then I will have the most legendary wipeout of all time!
The way I figure it, I win either way. That "Go for It!" attitude is in our
DNA as surfers, and more often than not, we come shooting out the tube
with our arms held up high. "Going For It!" is a metaphor for life that has
served surfers well!

HOW TO READ A SCREENPLAY

A screenplay is not a novel. A screenplay is a set of directions for the filmmaker to tell a story on screen. As you are reading the story, transport yourself into the "Director's Chair", and visualize how <u>You</u> would film the scenes of the movie. This is <u>Your</u> chance to live in the mind of a filmmaker!

A screenplay adheres to strict formatting rules. The primary rule to understand is, 1 page of a script is equal to 1 minute of a movie. Therefore, a screenplay that is 120 pages is equivalent to a 2-hour movie. This 1 page-a-minute concept is important. You do not have the luxury of describing characters and story descriptions at length. It is very brief and to the point. A character is usually described in a few sentences, not pages or even chapters as in a novel. It is up to the filmmaker (<u>You</u>) to visually make the characters and scenes come alive on the screen. A description can be brief because "A Picture Tells a Thousand Words". The challenge of a screenplay is to be able to tell a complete story within the 120-page guideline and make it interesting and engaging. I feel like I have achieved this with "The Bond Between Surfers" and I hope you enjoy my story.

A Side Note: I know have taken some "Liberties" with the strict formatting rules in order to convert it into a book format, but I also wanted to make it enjoyable for the reader who has never read a screenplay before. Therefore, the 1 page a minute rule <u>does not apply</u> to the book version since a screenplay is in written on an 8½x11 inch page and the book is written on a 6x9 inch page.

I have the **TRADITIONAL FORMATTED SCREENPLAY**, which is **126 PAGES**, available for any filmmaker who may have a serious interest in making this into a feature length film. I am open for collaboration and you can contact me at my website www.tbbsurf.com or scan the QR Code.

GLOSSARY OF FILM TERMS

Here are a few definitions of jargon used in the screenplay to help you better navigate the story.

INT. – Interior. This is a scene shot indoors.

EXT. – Exterior. This is a scene shot outdoors.

EXT. ANY BEACH – MORNING – This is an example of a scene description telling the filmmaker where to film. Outdoors - At the Beach - In the Morning. All scene descriptions have this format.

O.S. – Off Screen. The character is off screen but still part of the scene.

PASSAGE OF TIME – A montage of scenes depicting that time has passed in the story. It tells the viewer that time has passed instantly.

POV – Point Of View. This is when you see the scene through the character's eyes. You see what the character is seeing.

SERIES OF SHOTS – A montage of action scenes put together to enhance the story within the scene.

V.O. – Voice Over. This is a voice coming out of a mechanical device such as a telephone, or loudspeaker.

UNNAMED CHARACTERS – An example of an unnamed character is Surfer #1. All unnamed characters are assigned a number. Example Surfer#1, Surfer #2, Surfer #3, etc.

THE BOND BETWEEN SURFERS

By

Mark Rebscher

Graphics By

Mark Rebscher

1976

BAJAN
SURFBOARDS

BECOMING A SURFER

FADE IN:

EXT. ANY BEACH - MORNING (1976)

A mother and her child are on the beach. They are near the shoreline. The ocean is exceptionally clear and blue with golden highlights from the sunrise. Glassy 6-to-8-foot waves are breaking one after the other. They are the only ones on the beach. ART DURAND is a 10-year-old boy, trim in figure, mop style 70's haircut, and has an easy-going demeanor. He is like a sponge soaking up the nature around him and all the experiences life has to offer. He is wearing cutoff jeans with frayed edges which doubles as a bathing suit.

Art is completely enthralled in the sand castle he is building. SALLY DURAND is sitting in a lawn chair underneath a beach umbrella. She is reading a book and occasionally looks at her son with a loving gaze.

Art is sitting close to the water's edge. He is making his castle, when THE SURFER approaches as a towering figure and stands next to Art. He has an unzipped "beavertail wetsuit top" which reveals his ripped surfer muscles and a pukka shell necklace. He is the quintessential 70's surfer, with sun bleached mid-length hair, and a dark tan. He has a 1970's light blue single fin surfboard with a picture of a large wave airbrushed on the deck. He sets the surfboard in the sand next to Art.

Art stops building his sandcastle and watches with curiosity as
The Surfer waxes his board. The Surfer then stares out into the ocean, as he would stare into the eyes of a girl he has fallen in love with. He picks up the surfboard, and gives Art a smile and nod.

The Surfer enters the water. He picks up speed, vaults horizontally belly first onto his board, and glides on the water. He effortlessly begins to paddle out to the waves. He is at peace with nature and the universe. Through his actions, he pulls Art into his world... <u>The surfing world.</u>

The Surfer is paddling out towards the lineup. The 6-to-8-foot waves in front of him are pitching out perfectly with an offshore spray. As the whitewater approaches, he sinks himself and the board underwater. As the turbulence of the wave passes over him, he ascends back to the surface. With one long whipping motion from his head, he flicks his hair back, lets out a relaxing breath of air, and continues paddling.

Art is sitting on the beach in front of his sand castle. He is mesmerized by The Surfer. Watching intently, Art never takes his eyes off of him.

The Surfer drops into an 8-foot wave, does a long-drawn-out bottom turn, and maneuvers his board to the middle of the wave. He moves slightly to the center of the surfboard. The surfboard picks up speed as he glides down the middle of the face. He heads for the trough, does another bottom turn, heads straight up the wave, and does an off-the-lip. The off-the-lip sends a rooster tail spray. The wave begins to pitch out, and he slows his board down. He sets up for a tube ride as the water pitches over him. He is completely covered by the wave. All of a sudden, he comes shooting out of the tube like a cannon ball! The Surfer exits the wave and paddles back out.

Sally lifts her head from out of the book. She glances over to Art, who is staring out into the ocean. She looks towards the ocean to see what has captivated Art's attention so deeply. She sees The Surfer trimming down another wave. Sally looks back at Art and realizes that is what he is staring at.

The Surfer is sitting on his board in the ocean. He is looking at a line of pelicans gliding by with wings spread wide. The pelicans are surfing the air currents caused by the offshore spray of the waves. The Surfer senses a wave approaching and looks at the oncoming set. With an ecstatic look, he glances back up at the pelicans one last time, then back down to his surfboard. He drops in and surfs the wave with grace and elegance.

As time passes, The Surfer catches a final wave, rides it to perfection, and paddles to shore. He walks past a washed away sand castle, stops, and looks at Art. Art looks up at him in awe. The Surfer smiles at Art and gives him another nod. This is the seminal moment when…

Art knows he wants to be a surfer.

DISSOLVE TO:

BAJAN
SURFBOARDS
SEEK
HARMONY
OPEN
BAJAN
SURFBOARDS

FIRST SURFBOARD

EXT. PARKING LOT - DAY

A Pontiac Bonneville pulls up to a gravel parking lot. In front of the parking lot is a building with bleached wood siding. Attached to the building is a circular logo that displays the Barbados flag's trident, yellow, and blue colors. The word BAJAN (Bay-jun) is above the trident and SURFBOARDS is below the trident. There are boards displayed in the window showing the Bajan Surfboards logo. Art hurriedly jumps out of the car and Sally follows.

> SALLY
> I don't understand, why you want to
> come here?

> ART
> Come on mom, I gotta show you
> something.

INT. BAJAN SURFBOARDS - DAY

Sally and Art enter the surf shop. JOE MONTGOMERY is the owner of the surf shop. Joe is one of many proud Black Surfers who originates from the island of Barbados. He is in his 50's with short hair and a gray beard. He is wearing a T-shirt with the Bajan Surfboards logo on it, shorts, and a pair of leather flip flops. Joe is the most respected surfer in the area. He is a wise sage who has all the answers to the meaning of life. He is sitting on a stool behind the glass counter, which contains surfing items. Joe is reading a "Surfer Magazine". He looks up at Sally & Art.

> JOE
> Welcome to Bajan (Bay-jun)
> Surfboards!... Wuz d word!

Art, puzzled, looks at Joe and says nothing.

> JOE
> How are you doing? What's happening?

> ART
> Oh... I'm good. Just came in to look at
> the surfboards.

Joe with a fatherly glance looks at Art as if he is talking to his own son.

> JOE
> Weren't you here the other day with your
> sister?

> ART
> (enthusiastically)
> Yeah! I really wanna get a surfboard.

Sally looks at Art a bit surprised. With a sheepish pleading glance, Art looks up at his mom and smiles.

> ART
> All I want is a surfboard. I've got some
> money saved up, and I'll work the rest off
> around the house.

> SALLY
> I don't know...

> ART
> Just look at the one I picked out.

Art, Sally, and Joe head to the back of the shop where about 25 Bajan Surfboards are hanging and leaning against the walls in a rack. There are numerous photos of surfers pasted all over the walls. Art pulls out a shiny new single fin surfboard. The price says $235.

> SALLY
Two-hundred and thirty-five dollars!

Joe looks at Sally, then Art.

> JOE
Have you ever surfed before?

> ART
No.

> JOE
Well, this is a top of the line, high performance surfboard. It's made for the most experienced surfers only.

Joe acknowledges Sally's price concern with wink and a nod.

> ART
> (looking disheartened)
Oh.

Joe takes Art over to the used board section. There are a bunch of old dinged, discolored, and abused boards. Joe pulls out a single fin from the racks. The foam is brown and there are quite a few dings on it.

> JOE
This is what you need. It's more stable. You'll be able to learn faster on this board. Once you get your basics down, then come see me and get a new board.

> ART
Yeah, but look how beat up it is.

SALLY
Honey, it doesn't look all that bad.

Art looking bummed out, starts checking out the other beat up used boards. He pulls a few of them out of the rack, but nothing interests him. Joe, who has taken a liking to Art, sizes up the situation. Joe stands there and thinks quietly for a second.

JOE
Wait a minute... I've got just the board
for you!

Joe walks OFF SCREEN into the back of his office. Sally and Art wait next to the surfboards. To pass the time, Art starts looking at the pictures on the wall.

PICTURE #1 - Caption reads "1975 Bajan Surf Team". It's a team photo. There are 30 plus large and small trophies laid out in front of the group of surfers. The picture looks like you just came back from a fishing trip. The entire catch is laid out in front of the surf team, but instead of fish they are trophies.

PICTURE #2 - A series of old yellowed newspaper clippings and ripped out pages of magazines. They are younger pictures of Joe and other Black surfers when he lived in Barbados. These pictures establish Joe's credibility and history as a surfer. Each picture has a caption on them such as, "Joe Montgomery, Barbados National Champ" ... "Barbados 1st Surfing Laureate, Joe Montgomery" ... "Joe Montgomery Takes the Surfing World By Storm" ... "The Pride of Barbados, Joe Montgomery". As Art is reading the clippings, Joe comes ON SCREEN with a light blue single fin surfboard.

JOE
This is one of my team rider's... He just
traded it in on a new board.

Joe sets the tail of the surfboard down on the carpet and holds the nose with his hand. The bottom of the board has the words Bajan Surf Team on it. Art glances back at the pictures on the wall, then at Joe.

ART
I'm going to be on the surf team one day.

JOE
That's the spirit!

Joe spins the board around so that the deck is facing Art. All of a sudden Art's eyes light up as he recognizes the picture of the large wave airbrushed on the light blue deck. He realizes this is the same board that The Surfer was riding on the beach the other day!

JOE
Well... What do you think?

ART
(excitedly)
You'll sell me this one!

JOE
Sure, I'll even give you a leash and some
wax with it.

SALLY
How much do you want for it?

JOE
How about seventy-five dollars.

Sally glances at Art's overjoyed face and grins.

SALLY
How much money do you have?

ART
I've got 11 dollars and 53 cents.

> SALLY
> Tell you what. If you help your dad with
> the yardwork for the rest of the summer,
> we'll call it even.

> ART
> I will, I promise. Thanks, mom!

Sally, Art, and Joe walk up to the counter. Art hands Sally a bunch of crumpled up bills and a handful of change. She takes the money and combines it with hers. She then gives the money to Joe. Joe hands Art two bars of wax and a bungee leash.

> JOE
> You're going to make a great surfer.

Art enthusiastically checks out his new surfboard. For a surfer, getting your first surfboard is a special defining once in a lifetime moment. Joe looks at Art, grins, and shakes his head. Joe walks around the counter to the T-shirt rack. He pulls out a small T-shirt with the Bajan Surfboards logo on it. He tosses it on Art and the T-shirt drapes his head. Art grabs it and looks at it.

> JOE
> We have a stoked surfer's special today.
> All stoked surfers, get a free t-shirt.

> ART
> Stoked?

> JOE
> You know... Happy, ecstatic, thrilled...
> Stoked!

> ART
> Thanks! Mr...

JOE
Montgomery, but everyone calls me Joe.

ART
I'm Art, and I don't think there's anyone
more <u>stoked</u> than me right now.

Art picks up the surfboard, bungee leash, and wax. Since the board is much bigger than him, he struggles to carry it out the door. As he is walking towards the door, he drops the bars of wax from his hand one at a time. He then drops the T-shirt. He is unable to pick them up due to the bulkiness of the surfboard. Sally picks them up behind him. Finally, the leash is the last item to drop, and he is left just carrying the surfboard out the door….

DISSOLVE TO:

WIPEOUT KING!

BEST FRIENDS

EXT. BEACH - DAY

A makeshift picnic table sits on the sand in front of the surf break. A few surfers, whose ages range from 12-20, are hanging out on the picnic table looking at the 2–3-foot surf rolling in. All the surfers look and dress as if they have walked out of a 1976 "Surfer Magazine". Art and a few other surfers are in the water.

EXT. OCEAN - DAY

Art is awkwardly sitting on his surfboard. A 3-foot wave nears. Art lays on his board with the nose sticking up in the air and paddles to catch the wave. It is obvious he is still learning. The wave catches Art, who is in the wrong position, and hurls him over the falls in a major wipeout.

                         ART
          Whoooaaa!

Art disappears underneath the water. Then his head pops up out of the water as he gasps for air. Just as he grabs a breath, another wave pummels him. Again, he disappears and reappears gasping for air. Once out of the impact zone, he regains his composure, clumsily gets back on his surfboard, and paddles back out.

LEDGE MAJORS paddles by Art to give him some encouragement and pointers. Ledge, a fashion designer, is the androgynous alter ego of Craig Parker. In a similar way that Ziggy Stardust is the androgynous alter ego of David Bowie. Ledge's persona and outfits are one of a very stylish and sleek surfer look, blended together with the glam rock style of the 70's. Ledge is 18 years old and a heroic figure that has the ability to sooth souls and always comes to the rescue of the surfing crew. Everyone loves, respects, and accepts Ledge just as Ledge is.

LEDGE

Grade A wipeout. The judges give you a
9.25 on that one. It would've been a 10.
But when you came up for air, there
wasn't enough water coming out of your
nose.

ART

Thanks Ledge, I'll try harder next time.

LEDGE

Good man... Look, when you're
paddling, you need to have your body
further up on the board so the nose
doesn't stick out as much. That'll make
the board more streamlined in the water.

ART

Ok.

LEDGE

Also, keep your legs together, they're too
spread out, it's slowing you down...
Put'm together like this.

Ledge shows him the correct form, and Art tries to copy it.

LEDGE

It's a little weird at first, but you'll get the
hang of it. Have fun paddling through
the whitewater.

Ledge paddles back out to the lineup, leaving Art behind. As a wave is
about to break in front of Ledge, Ledge looks back at Art.

LEDGE
Remember, hold onto your board no
matter what!

Ledge easily duck dives the wave. Art, on the other hand, comes up to the surface, upside down, holding onto his board, and gasping for air. In the FOREGROUND, Ledge looks back at Art.

LEDGE
(shouts enthusiastically)
STOKEN!!!!!!!

Art smiles and is proud that he is still holding onto his surfboard.

CUT TO:

Art is back out at the lineup when he notices VIA FRANCO sitting on her yellow surfboard. Via is the same age as Art, 10 years old. She is from South America. Via has that magical outgoing personality that makes anyone instantly like her and happily follow her to the ends of the earth. Everyone always wants to be around Via and she is the life of the party.

Trying to act cool, Art looks at Via with trepidation. He then sees a wave off in the distance and starts paddling for it. He drops down the face of the wave as if he is riding a sled on his stomach. When he gets to the bottom of the wave, he stands up in an uncoordinated fashion. Art rides the wave with little control, then falls off.

ART
Yeeeeew! That was Rad! What a wave!

Via tentatively catches the next wave. She does a carbon copy of the ride Art just had. Art watches her ride the wave. Via clumsily falls off close to where Art is floating. Both of them stoked on their rides, look at each other.

                    ART
Kinda' looks like we're in the same boat,
huh?

                    VIA
More like a sinking ship.

                    ART
Yeah, I got the wipe outs wired.

                    VIA
As my big brother says, "Be the best at
whatever you do". So, you can be the
wipeout king! And I'll be the underwater
breath holder champ!

                    ART
Champions we'll be!

Art and Via look at each other and have become instant friends. They get
on their boards and paddle back out to the lineup. A wave approaches and
pummels both of them. They come up to the surface upside down holding
their boards and gasping for air. They look at each other and start
laughing.

EDUARDO FRANCO is Via's 14-year-old brother. He paddles by Art
and Via.

                    EDUARDO
Looking good!

Eduardo in a friendly manner splashes some water at Via and paddles off.

                    VIA
Thanks Eduardo!

Via proudly looks at Art.

> VIA

That's my big brother.

Art and Via get back on their boards, and proceed to paddle back out to the lineup.

> CUT TO:

> ART

So, what's your name?

> VIA

Vianey, but my friends call me Via.
What's yours?

> ART

Art... Are you here for the day?

> VIA

No, I just moved here from the
Galapagos Islands in Ecuador.

> ART

Galapagos Islands! How the heck did
you end up here?

> VIA

Both of my parents are Oceanographers.
They measure the effects of changing
ocean temperatures on coral reefs.

> ART

Wow...

> VIA

Their research is expanding to this part of
the world and now they work here at the
University.

                    ART
That's so Rad!

                    VIA
Rad?

                    ART
Radical! Amazing! You're just like
Jacques Cousteau. I live...

Art stops talking and hurriedly turns around as a wave begins to break and takes off on it.

He goes over the falls once again. Art comes up and takes a breath of air. In the FOREGROUND, Via is laughing. She looks at Art and raises her arms.

                    VIA
Champions we'll be!

Art smiles and begins to laugh.

                              DISSOLVE TO:

GROMS
BAJAN
SURFBOARDS
WILL RULE
THE
WORLD!

GROMS WILL RULE THE WORLD!

EXT. STREET – DAY

A CLOSEUP of cards in the spokes of a spinning bicycle wheel are making loud snapping noises. PAN OUT to Art and Via in a hotly competitive race. Attached to each bike are their surfboards horizontally strapped onto homemade surf racks. Art is in the lead with Via closing in fast behind him.

Joe is sitting outside of Bajan Surfboards reading a "Surfer Magazine" when he hears the clicking and clacking noises of the bikes. He looks up to see Art and Via rounding the corner pedaling as hard as they can. Art sees Joe and waves, which slows him down. It's as if Art has completely forgotten about the race

ART
Yeeeew! Joe!

Via with a determination to win, seizes the moment to pass Art. Watching and understanding what is unfolding, Joe signals Art to pedal faster! Art smiles at Joe one last time and begins to accelerate but his competitive drive is lost. They arrive to the beach and Via is the victor.

VIA
Yeah! I beat you by a mile! It wasn't
even close.

Art becomes distracted as he looks at a nearby bush. He pedals closer to see a large caterpillar on a leaf. He picks it up and lets it crawl on his hand.

VIA
My Abuelita can pedal faster than you!

Via is still boasting about her win when she realizes that Art is oblivious to what she is saying. Via rolls her eyes, shakes her head, and puts her arms up in the air. She gives up knowing that Art's attention is now consumed by the caterpillar and her victory celebration has become meaningless and hopeless.

                                                            CUT TO:

EXT. BEACH - DAY

Art and Via are walking their bikes in the sand. In the FOREGROUND, is the makeshift picnic table with a bunch of surfers sitting and standing around it. Surfboards are lying all over the place. Ledge and 5 other younger surfers (male and female) whose ages range from 10-15 are hanging out. TUNA is also there. He is 20 years old, tall, full of muscles, and ripped like a tuna. Tuna is like the big older brother that picks on you because you are much smaller, but at the same time he would always protect you in a bad situation. Everyone likes Tuna. He defends the close-knit surf crew from the dangers of the outside world.

All the surfers are in bathing suits and some still have t-shirts on. They are all watching the 6-foot waves breaking in front of them. Art and Via methodically take their boards out of the bicycle racks and lean the bikes on the picnic table. Art looks at Ledge. Ledge is wearing a bikini type top with curved shoulder pads and multicolored swim trunks.

ART
Ledge. Totally diggin the outfit!

LEDGE
Yeah, it's one of my latest designs. It's
called, "If Ziggy Stardust was a Surfer".

                    ART
Nice!!!!

                   LEDGE
I can't believe you two are just getting
here. The waves are cookin! You've
missed the morning sesh.

                    VIA
              (proudly)
That's what you think, we dawned
patrolled it.

                    ART
Yeah, we were surfing before the sun was
up. This is our 2nd session of the day.

                    VIA
              (jokingly)
Art was sleeping in. I made it here 15
minutes before he did.

                    ART
              (jokingly)
Oh Yeah. We'll see who's the earliest
tomorrow... Kook.

(Note: The competition/banter to see who can get to the beach the earliest
is a recurring theme throughout the movie)

Tuna teases Art and Via in a disgusted yet joking manner.

                   TUNA
What a bunch of grommets!

Tuna then looks at the rest of the younger surfers.

TUNA
In fact, you're all a bunch of grommets!

15-YEAR-OLD SURFER
Hey Tuna! Watch who you're calling a
grommet.   I ain't no grommet!

LEDGE
You can be 15 and still be a grommet. It's
more a state of mind, than how old you
are.

TUNA
You're a grommet til we say so! That
goes for all you little knuckleheads.

15-YEAR-OLD SURFER
(Challenging Tuna)
Who are you calling a knucklehead?

TUNA
You! You little grommet!

VIA
Hey! I think there's enough grommets
here to take you, Tuna.

Tuna smiles with bravado and confidence.

TUNA
Bring it on! I'll smush all of you like
sand crabs and feed you to the sharks.

Via with a grin of a leader, looks at Art and the other 5 younger surfers.
Art and the 5 younger surfers look at Via and start grinning.

VIA
Let's get'em!

Via, Art, and the 5 younger surfers all jump on Tuna at once. They are laughing and giggling as they manage to take Tuna face down in the sand. They are throwing harmless little grommet punches wherever they can, in the legs, arms, back, and ribs.

                              TUNA
                           (laughing)
                    Is this all you've got!

Art and Via get a grip of his head. They start mashing Tuna's face in the sand. This makes Tuna mad and he loses his temper.

Ledge can be seen in the FOREGROUND laughing uncontrollably as Tuna gets clobbered by all the grommets.

There is a 10-YEAR-OLD BOY with thick coke-bottle glasses on his face. During the brawl, his glasses get accidently knocked off his head. In SLOW MOTION, you can see a CLOSEUP of the glasses tumbling through the air. The Boy instinctively reaches for them and misses. Tuna uses the opportunity to throw The Boy off his body.

In order to avoid the wrath of Tuna, all the groms panic, instantly jump off him, and scatter like cockroaches about to be stepped on.

This leaves The Boy alone in the sand searching for his glasses.

Tuna has sand all over his face and furiously gets up. He sees The Boy and picks him up.

Everyone is laughing and giving cat calls.

                              VIA
                    Groms will rule the world!

                          GROMMET #1
                    Yeah, beat it, Tuna! Before we stick you
                    in a can!

Tuna tosses The Boy into the sand, grinds his face in it, picks him up, and throws him in the water. The Boy, bummed out and having a hard time seeing, stumbles out of the water.

THE BOY'S POV - BLURRED VISION

A set of blurred eyeglasses comes into the POV of The Boy. As the blurred eyeglasses get closer, the screen comes back into focus. As if, the glasses are being put on The Boys face to see again. The Boy sees Ledge putting on his glasses.

EXT. BEACH - DAY

Ledge as if in a coronation ceremony for knights, proudly addresses The Boy.

> LEDGE
> For your valiant efforts to rid the world
> of De-Evolution... Your name shall now
> be... DEVO!...

Ledge knights The Boy with hand motions.

> LEDGE
> Stand Tall... Spud Boy!

This makes The Boy proud. From now on THE BOY is known as DEVO.

> DEVO
> Thanks Ledge.

At the picnic table, all the grommets are celebrating their brief victory over Tuna.

Moments later, a surfer about 50 years old walks by the picnic table. He is carrying an old beat-up longboard from the 60's underneath his arm.

ART
I didn't know people from the old folks
home surfed.

All the grommets laugh amongst themselves. The older surfer turns his
head around, establishes eye contact with Art, and smiles. He turns his
head back around and continues walking to the beach. Art realizing what
he said was wrong, stops laughing, and stares at the older surfer as he
walks to the water. The other surfers, on the other hand, are still cutting
up.

GROMMET #2
I hope he doesn't lose his false teeth
when he goes over the falls.

Art with an irritated look, nudges Grommet #2.

ART
Come on man... Let's go surfing.

DISSOLVE TO:

<u>A PASSAGE OF TIME</u>

(NOTE: All passages of time throughout the movie will showcase THE ICONIC SURFBOARD of that year. Illustrating the evolution of the surfboard)

<u>Year 1977</u> - **7'4" AIPA STINGER.** Single fin, yellow with red flames on the deck.

<u>Year 1978</u> - **7'6" LIGHTNING BOLT.** Single fin, pin tail, all red with a yellow lightning bolt.

<u>Year 1979</u> - **8'6" YATER SPOON.** From the movie "Apocalypse Now". Single fin, noserider, military pea green, with the U.S. Military 1st Calvary Air Mobile logo on the deck.

<u>Year 1980</u> - **6'2" "MR" SUPERMAN LOGO.** Twin fin, single wing swallow tail, red deck with 1 rail blue and 1 rail green.

<u>Year 1981</u> - **5'8" MCCOY LAZORZAP PHASE I.** Single fin, tear drop design, black & white checkers in "V" formation with red and blue deck.

FADE TO:

1982

PLANET
BLUE TUBE

PLANET BLUE TUBE

This is an **<u>ANIMATED SCENE</u>**. Art is now 16 years old and is having an epic surfing dream. It's set in the future and is every surfer's fantasy dream come true!

INT. BEDROOM - MORNING

Art is sleeping in his ANIMATED futuristic 16-year-old surfer style bedroom. His room is adorned with all sorts of surfing posters, surfboards, etc.

Art wakes up bleary eyed and looks at his 6-inch-wide wristband console on his left forearm. He gets very excited, jumps out of bed, puts on his bathing suit, and t-shirt with a futuristic "Bajan Surfboards" logo on it. He grabs his rocket propelled surfboard with mini jet engines attached to each side of the tail of the surfboard and hurriedly leaves his bedroom.

EXT. HOUSE DRIVEWAY - MORNING

Art is strapping his rocket propelled surfboard on the roof racks of a sleek looking personal spaceship the size of a car.

INT. SPACESHIP - MORNING

Art is in the cockpit programming the coordinates on a touch screen. CLOSEUP - The words "PLANET BLUE TUBE" appear on the screen. Then the words "Distance: 27 Light Years" appear on the screen.

EXT. HOUSE DRIVEWAY - MORNING

Art's spaceship with the surfboard attached to roof racks, hovers, turns around, and blasts off!

INT. SPACESHIP - DARKNESS OF SPACE

As Art is looking into the darkness of space. He starts talking to the cockpit computer.

                    ART
          Warp Speed 44.

                    COMPUTER VOICE (V.O.)
          Understood... Music Selection?

                    ART
          Queen... "Flash Gordon OST, Battle
          Theme".

                    COMPUTER VOICE (V.O.)
          Understood...

Surround Sound speakers mechanically rise out of the dashboard of the spaceship. Art with an adventurous smile, puts on some cool sunglasses, and leans back in the seat. Art's right hand is on a throttle and slams it forward 12 inches. WHAM! The spaceship goes into hyperspace as the <u>wildly action-packed music</u> by Queen begins to blast out of the speakers.

                                        CUT TO:

ART'S POV - SPACE

A dot appears in the middle of the blackness of space. As the dot gets larger and larger, it reveals a giant completely blue ocean planet. As Art's spaceship gets closer, one tiny brown dot appears in the blue ocean. The spaceship gets even closer to reveal a single island surrounded by the vastness of the ocean. It's the only land mass on the entire planet. As the spaceship gets closer, the island gets larger, revealing a perfect right point break wave breaking on the whole left-hand side of the island. The waves are peeling for over 100 miles!

EXT. ISLAND - DAY

Art's rocket touches down on the island next to a solitary alien type palm tree. Art is checking out the waves. The waves are perfection! It's the type of wave every high school surfer would draw on their notebooks. At this point, it's unclear how big the waves are.

Art takes off his rocket propelled surfboard from the spaceship, puts it in the sand, and waxes the deck.

CUT TO:

EXT. OCEAN - DAY

A CLOSEUP of Art paddling to catch a wave. He catches the wave and starts to drop in. He presses a button on the 6-inch wristband console. The screen on the console says "Accelerate". The rocket boosters on the surfboard ignite and the jet propels him down the wave.

The camera PANS OUT to a wide angle shot to reveal a 300-foot wave! Art now becomes just a tiny spec as he rockets to the bottom.

Art is doing a sweeping bottom turn, heads back up, and does an off-the-lip which results in a 100-foot rooster tail spray. Art does a cutback and heads back to the breaking wave. He makes it to the top and floats down the wave curtain as it is pitching out.

He makes a stylish 45-degree erect bottom turn and heads up the wave. Art presses a button on the wrist console. The console screen says "Lift-Off". The camera PANS OUT to see Art as a tiny spec rocketing up the wave. He blasts out the top in a 200-foot aerial.

He comes back down into the wave and heads to the bottom. Art presses another button on the wrist console that reads "Stall". He puts his right hand in the face of the wave as a 300-foot cavernous tube surrounds him. He keeps getting deeper and deeper in the tube. 10 feet deep, 25 feet deep, 50 feet deep, 100 feet deep!

All of a sudden, a CAMERAMAN pops out of the face of the wave and snaps a picture of his ride. Art gives the cameraman the "Classic Peace Sign Pose" for the shot.

INSERT - "SURFER MAGAZINE" COVER SHOT

It's a full-page cover shot of Art deep in the tube. The caption reads, "EPIC PLANET BLUE TUBE".

BACK TO SCENE

Art presses a button and the wrist console says "Accelerate". He shoots out of the tube and back onto the face.

All of a sudden, a giant 200-foot SEA SERPENT comes out of the water and chases Art. The sea serpent is gaining on him. The sea serpent opens his mouth and is about to eat Art whole, like a piece of popcorn... When just at that moment, the animation goes FUZZY.

> VIA (V.O.)
> Art... Art... Wake up! Its been daylight for
> a half an hour now, and you're still
> snoozing. Get up you lazy, good-for-
> nothin' surf bum.

INT. ART'S BEDROOM - MORNING (SUMMER 1982)

The movie switches back to **LIVE ACTION**. Art's room is covered with posters of his surfing heroes, circa 1982. Today is Art's 16th birthday.

Via is jabbing Art's ribs with the nose of his twin fin surfboard. Art and Via are a bit taller, noticeably older, but still look like kids. Via is starting to have an 80's "New Wave" surf vibe about her. Art looks like a classic early 80's surfer. All the characters are now dressed like they just walked out of a 1982 "Surfer Magazine".

                    ART
          Hey... Hey... What'ya doing. I'm in the
          best dream of my life!

                    VIA
          You're sleeping in for a dream??? What's
          wrong with you!

Via keeps poking Art with his surfboard.

                    ART
          Ow... Ow... That hurts.

                    VIA
          We have surf to catch birthday boy.

                    ART
          Leave me alone. There's no waves today.
          It's flat, unrideable, even G.I. Joe
          couldn't surf today.

                    VIA
          That's no excuse. I heard The Cape is
          huge! We should be road tripping it.

                    ART
          Yeah, like how are we gonna get there?

                    VIA
          Minor details... I don't see why that
          should stop us. Get up! I gotta show you
          something!

ART
Might as well. My dream's ruined after
those flesh wounds you just gave me.

Art gets out of bed and walks into the bathroom. He is wearing a
Quiksilver bathing suit with stars all over them as pajamas. Via picks up
a "Surfer Magazine".

VIA
Finally... a picture of Debbie Beacham
surfing.

ART (O.S.)
Is that not the insanest off-the-lip you
ever saw! Do you think she pulled it off?

VIA
Yeah! She isn't world champ for
nothing... I'm gonna be world champ
one day...

ART (O.S.)
Dream on...

VIA
You wait and see!

Art comes out of the bathroom fully dressed.

ART
Now, what were you gonna show me?

VIA
Oh yeah...

Via tosses the magazine on the bed and they walk out of the bedroom.

DISSOLVE TO:

SURFING NOMADS

SURFING NOMADS

EXT. PORCH - MORNING

Art and Via walk out the front door onto the porch. In the driveway is a
1971 dark green, slightly rusted, and slightly dented VW camper bus with
a big red bow on the windshield. Art's parents and sister come out from
behind the bus cheering.

                    FAMILY & VIA
          Happy 16th birthday!

                    ART
               (looking surprised and stunned)
          No way... For me?

                    SALLY
          It's for you...

                    ART
          Really, for me?

                    FATHER
          It's all yours.

                    ART
          Wow! This is the best birthday present
          ever! You guys are the greatest!

Art Walks over and hugs his whole family. Everybody is stoked and
happy. Via walks over to the VW bus.

                    VIA
          You've gotta check out the inside.

Art walks over to the bus and Via opens the sliding door.

INT. VW BUS - MORNING

Art and Via go inside, and Art's family peers through the windows. Via pops the top of the VW bus so they can stand inside.

                    ART
          This thing's so rad!

Art looks around the inside and notices some of his clothes, Via's surfboard, blankets, groceries, lantern's, camping equipment, etc.

                    ART
          Hey, this looks like it's loaded for a trip.

                    VIA
          It is! I packed it myself. We're going to
          The Cape on our first surf safari.

                    ART
          Seriously! I'm so stoked!

                    VIA
          Yeah, my brother's gonna go with us.
          He's been there before and knows the
          way... We'll camp out and live in the
          bus!

                    ART
               (Magical adventurous tone)
          Like Surfing Nomads...

                    VIA
          I call top bunk!

                    ART
          You got it!

Art and Via get out of the VW bus.

> VIA
> Everything is ready to go. All ya' gotta
> do is get your surfboard and pass the
> driving test. The way I figure it. We'll
> be on the road by 10 am. We should be
> there by dark, and tomorrow we'll be
> surfing 8-to-10-foot perfection! Yeeeew!

> ART
> Yeeeew! We're going to the Cape!

Art and Via slap each other "five". Art puts his arm around his father and his father does the same thing. Everyone walks inside the house to eat breakfast.

> SISTER
> (tired and cranky)
> Now that he's got his car, can I please go
> back to bed!

DISSOLVE TO:

INT. MOVING VW BUS - DAY

Art is driving down the road, Via is in the passenger seat, and Eduardo is sitting in the back.

> VIA
> See, I told you that driving test was cake.
> It's a good thing you used your dad's car.

> ART
> Tell me about it, the stick shift in the bus
> is impossible.

Art tries to downshift and the gears start grinding. Eduardo is seen cringing with his hands over his ears. Art finally succeeds in downshifting.

                    ART
          One last stop and we are on the road.

Art makes a left-hand turn and pulls into Bajan Surfboards.

EXT. BAJAN SURFBOARDS - DAY

Joe is outside sitting in a lawn chair reading a "Surfer Magazine". Art, Via, and Eduardo jump out of the VW bus.

                    JOE
          Happy Birthday, Art. I see you got your
          present.

                    ART
          What? You knew about it too?

                    JOE
          Yeah, it's my neighbor's old bus. He's
          been wanting to sell it for a while. I told
          your mom about it... and there you go...
          What are you doing here? I thought
          you'd be long gone by now.

                    ART
          We came to get some wax... Then we're
          outta here.

                    JOE
          Go on in and get some.

Art and Via go inside to get some wax. Joe remains seated. He picks up a cup of coffee, and some sugar packets. Joe tears open the packets and empties the contents into the coffee. He then picks up a rusty old screwdriver, sticks the screwdriver in the cup, and stirs his coffee. Joe sets down the screwdriver. Eduardo walks up to Joe. Joe puts down the cup of coffee, stands up, and with a big smile shakes Eduardo's hand.

JOE
¿Hola cómo vas? Todo bien?

EDUARDO
¡Qué buena onda verte, bro!

JOE
¿Estás ocupado con esos dos, no es así?

EDUARDO
(laughing and joking)
Eh! No te preocupes! Si se ponen
difíciles, los amarro en el techo del auto.

JOE
(laughing and joking)
Ok bro, pero asegúrate de que no dañen
las tablas de surf.

Joe and Eduardo are still laughing. Art and Via, each with a handful of surf wax, come back outside. They walk over to Joe.

VIA
Thanks Joe.

ART
Yeah, thanks Joe. Especially, for telling
my mom about the bus.

JOE
Da Easy (Bajan for you're welcome) ...
But there's one thing you can do for me...

ART & VIA
What's that.

JOE
Catch a wave for me.

VIA
You know it!

Art and Via jump into the VW bus. Eduardo shakes Joe's hand and gets in the bus. Art starts it up and tries shifting into reverse. Joe is cringing with every grind of the gears. Art finally pops it into reverse and the bus starts backing up, Art and Via stick their heads out the window.

VIA
We're gonzo!

ART
Yeeeew!

JOE
Chat you later. (Bajan for bye)

ART'S POV - THROUGH THE BUS FRONT WINDOW.

Joe shakes his head and waves. They pull out and head down the street. They spot Ledge walking and excitedly pull over.

ART
Ledge!!!

LEDGE
I thought that was you. What's up with
the bus?

ART
I just got it for my birthday!

                    VIA
Yeah! We're off to The Cape!

                  LEDGE
          (Saying it like it is a very
           special and sacred event)
Aaaah... Your virgin trip to The Cape...

                  LEDGE
          (a bit more serious)
You know it breaks a lot bigger and
harder up there.

                   ART
We've heard the stories.

                    VIA
We can handle it.

                  LEDGE
Well, as much as I hate to say it. You're
not groms anymore. Go for it! And don't
hold back... We've got a reputation to
uphold around here... So don't let us
down in the surf!

Art committed, looks at Ledge.

                   ART
We won't!

                                    CUT TO:

ART'S POV - THROUGH THE BUS FRONT WINDOW.

Art sees Devo and another surfer walking down the street and drives towards them. Devo is now 16, still wearing thick black glasses, and has black curly poofed out hair. Via sticks her head out of the bus as they come up behind Devo

                    VIA
          Hey Devo!

EXT. STREET - DAY

Devo turns around to see who is calling for him. Via with her head out of the bus, yells, as they pass by.

                    VIA
          SO LONG SUCKERS!

Devo looks in bewilderment as the bus passes by. He's confused as to why Art is driving a bus and Via is yelling out the window. Devo is clueless as to where they are going.

                                        CUT TO:

A SERIES OF SHOTS

A) Via has her arm out the window. She is surfing the air currents with her hand doing off-the-lips and cutbacks. The camera PANS OUT to the VW bus driving down the road with the ocean in the background.

B) The VW bus is winding through a forest on the edge of a mountain. On the righthand side you can see the ocean about 300 feet below. It stretches to the horizon.

C) Eduardo is driving, Art is crashed out in the passenger seat, and Via is drawing waves and sketches of her holding a big trophy with the caption "World Champ".

D) It is dark. All you can see is the full moon, the headlights, and a silhouette of the VW bus moving down a dirt road.

E) The VW bus is parked. The camper top is popped. The only light is a smoldering campfire and the moon. The only sounds are the crashing waves. Art, Via, and Eduardo are fast asleep.

DISSOLVE TO:

WAX PEOPLE

WAX PEOPLE

EXT. RIVER BANK - SUNRISE

The dark green VW bus with its popped top sits silently at the edge of a river mouth. In the FOREGROUND, is an eroded river bank which empties out into the ocean, a tree lined "U" shaped cove, and about 10-to-12-foot waves breaking.

CUT TO:

Art sits cross legged at the edge of the eroded river bank, watching the sunrise and the waves breaking in the FOREGROUND. He is next to the campfire drinking hot chocolate.

INT. VW BUS - SUNRISE

Via wakes up in her bunk which is in the top section of the VW bus. She looks at the waves through a little screened-in window.

> VIA
> (to herself)
> It's firing!

Via notices Art sitting next to the fire in a meditative state.

> VIA
> (to herself)
> Dang it!

Via scurries out of the top bunk, jumps to the floor, scoots around her sleeping brother, and exits the VW bus.

EXT. RIVER BANK - SUNRISE

Via, with a small box in her hand, walks up to Art who is sitting next to the fire. Art with a cocky grin looks up at Via.

                    ART
          There's a pot of hot chocolate near the
          fire.

                    VIA
               (defeated)
          Ok... Just go ahead and say it.

                    ART
          What?

                    VIA
          Just say it.

                    ART
               (sarcastically)
          Oh... You mean that you basically slept
          the whole morning away.

                    VIA
               (defeated)
          Yeah...

                    ART
          And we came hundreds of miles to surf
          and all you can to do is sleep.

Via looks at Art and acknowledges her defeat, then gets over it.

                    VIA
          Yeah, yeah... Now gimmie some of that
          hot chocolate.

Art and Via both look at each other, smile, and laugh.

                    ART
          The waves are goin off. They're some of
          the biggest waves I've ever seen.

Art points to the left-hand side of the river mouth.

                    ART
          Look how hollow it is. That's the spot
          Joe was telling me about. He said, "This
          is where you'll learn to be a great tube
          rider" ...

                    VIA
              (hypnotized)
          What an insane wave.

Via looks at Art and changes the subject.

                    VIA
          Remember when we were little, and Joe
          would pay us 5 bucks to scrape the old
          crusty wax off the used surfboards.

                                        FLASHBACK TO:

EXT. BAJAN SURFBOARDS - DAY (FLASHBACK)

Via and Art's DIALOGUE continues over the FLASHBACK. Art and
Via are 12 years old. They are outside of the surf shop scraping the wax
off of 10 used surfboards.

                    ART (V.O.)
          Yeah, we were like 12 and thought it was
          the coolest thing ever that Joe would ask
          us to scrape off the wax!

                    VIA (V.O.)
Do you remember those horribly
deformed figurines we made out of the
old crusty wax?

Art and Via smiling and laughing making deformed figures out of the gray
wax ball from the surfboards.

                    ART (V.O.)
I made a figurine that looked like you,
and you made a figurine that looked like
me...

                    VIA (V.O.)
                 (laughing)
They looked like mis-shapened zombies.
I stuck them together and said the
words...

                VIA (12 YEARS OLD)
   Friends forever!

                                    END FLASHBACK:

EXT. RIVER BANK - SUNRISE (PRESENT DAY)

Via hands Art a small box.

                    VIA
Happy 16th Birthday!

Art opens the box and reveals the deformed wax figurines. He looks at
Via with a big smile.

                    ART
Friends Forever!

Art and Via make eye contact with each other and acknowledge that they are, indeed, the best of friends!

CUT TO:

EXT. BEACH - MORNING

Art and Via are walking on the beach wearing full wetsuits. Each has a surfboard under their arms. They are winding their way through huge weathered logs and stumps that have been deposited here from the river. They reach the shoreline and strap their leashes to their ankle. Art and Via begin to paddle out. In the FOREGROUND, the hollow waves are breaking. Pelicans and other shorebirds are diving into the ocean, feeding off a school of fish. Art and Via duck dive the shore break and head for the surf.

ART'S POV - WAVE

Via is paddling as a huge wave breaks to the right. The wave pitches out, tubes, and spits out a plume of water. Via's facial features turn to excitement.

> VIA
> Did ya' see that tube! It's cookin'! Art!
> It's cookin'!

> ART
> Check out the one behind it! Radical!

> VIA
> I've died, and gone to heaven.

EXT. LINEUP - MORNING

Art and Via are sitting at the lineup. They have mastered the basics of surfing, but there is always more to learn. This is shown in their surfing styles.

                    ART
          Geez... It's a little bigger once you get
          out here.

                    VIA
          Tell me about it.

                    ART
          Well, let's go for it. The reputation of our
          home break is at stake.

                    VIA
          Here comes a set.

A 4 wave set marches in on the horizon. Every swell is a carbon copy
of the one behind it. As the first wave passes, Art and Via rise to the crest
and sink to the trough of the wave. The same thing happens again with
the second wave. Via looks at the third wave. She spins her board around
and paddles for the wave. She drops into a 10-footer. Looking a little
awkward she makes the bottom turn. The wave pitches out and lands right
on her head. She disappears underwater.

As Via surfaces, she looks at the next wave coming at her. Art is getting
ready to drop in.

VIA'S POV - WAVE

Via is watching Art drop into the wave. He also is looking a bit unsteady
making the bottom turn. The wave pitches out, but he is too far in front
of it to get tubed. Art speeds down the section as Via takes a breath and
dives underwater for safety.

VIA'S POV - UNDERWATER.

Via's hands are swimming to the bottom. The white turbulence gets a hold of her and spins her around like a washing machine. She begins to ascend and finally breaks through the surface gasping for air.

EXT. SURFACE - MORNING

Via quickly regains her composure.

> VIA
> Yeeeew! I love it!

VIA'S POV - BACK OF THE WAVE

Art is catapulted through the air, hooting, as the wave passes underneath him. Art lands in the water behind the wave. He retrieves his surfboard and paddles towards Via.

> ART
> This place is goin' off!

EXT. SURFACE - MORNING

Art and Via are side by side paddling back out to the lineup.

> ART
> How's your ride?

> VIA
> I got guillotined.

> ART
> Oooooo!

Art and Via arrive at the line up. A set wave appears on the horizon. Via looks at Art with a focused determination to conquer the world.

VIA

I'M ON IT!!!!!!

She spins around and paddles for the wave. Art and Via are now on a mission. They are taking on the waves with no fear or hesitation.

A SERIES OF SHOTS

A) Via drops into a wave, disappears under a curtain of water, and gets tubed.

B) Art does a sweeping bottom turn, stalls, and gets the barrel of his life!

C) Art and Via are hanging out at the lineup with 5 other surfers.

D) Eduardo catches a wave, gets tubed, and comes out.

E) Art, Via, and Eduardo are back at the campsite, eating a sandwich, and watching people surf in the FOREGROUND.

F) Art, Via, and Eduardo paddle back out to the lineup.

G) Art gets a deep barrel and comes out.

H) Via gets tubed and does a vertical off the lip.

I) The sunset approaches and silhouettes of surfers are sitting in the lineup. They are moving up and down with the crest and trough of the waves.

DISSOLVE TO:

SEEK
HARMONY

SOUL SURFER

INT. BAJAN SURFBOARDS - DAY

Art walks into Bajan Surfboards with a disheartened look about him. Joe is behind the counter. He is finishing up a sale with a customer. Joe notices the look on Art's face. Art is fumbling around the store waiting for the customer to leave. As the customer leaves, Joe's attention shifts to Art.

> JOE
> What's with the bummed face?

> ART
> Nothing.

> JOE
> Come on. I've seen that look before.

Art walks up to the counter and starts stacking bars of wax one on top of the other.

> ART
> (disheartened)
> I'm bummed 'cause... 'cause Via made
> the Bajan Surf Team, and I didn't!

Joe reaches behind the counter and gets a pen and a sheet of paper. He writes something on the paper.

> JOE
> Let's go check the waves.

> ART
> Ok.

Joe and Art walk outside. Joe tapes a sign to the door. The sign reads, "CHECKING THE SURF. BE BACK IN 15 MINUTES".

EXT. BEACH - DAY

Joe and Art are standing at the beach looking at the waves. In the FOREGROUND is the clear blue ocean with 2-to-4-foot peeling surf.

                    JOE
          Do you know what I regard as one of
          your finest qualities?

                    ART
          No, what?

                    JOE
          Transcendence... Your transcendence is
          far beyond your age. Far beyond most
          people on this earth.

Art has a puzzled look on his face.

                    ART
          I'm not sure I understand what you mean.

                    JOE
          There's a deep interconnection between
          your mind, the natural world, and the
          ocean... Your perception of the world is
          on a completely different level than the
          rest of us...

Joe looks around.

                    JOE
          What do you see?

                    ART
What do you mean by that?

                    JOE
Exactly what I said. Look around you...
Free and open your mind... Tell me what
do you see?

Art first looks at Joe a bit confused, but as their eyes lock, he understands
exactly what Joe is asking him. In a reflective and calm state, Art scans
the horizon.

                    ART
I see the ocean and the blue water rushing
through my veins. The sunlight
shimmering off the water's surface like
diamonds, and the offshore spray turning
into rainbows... I see the horizon ending
and the universe beginning.

                    JOE
Stunning! And how does it make you
feel?

                    ART
It has a cleansing effect on me... I feel
like I belong to the ocean... And the
ocean belongs to me... We are one...

Art looks at Joe as if he has figured out the meaning of life.

                    ART
It's paradise... Kinda' stupid, huh?

                    JOE
          No, not at all. Most surfers would have
          only seen the waves. They don't see the
          whole picture the way you do... Most
          surfers are <u>IN</u> the water, few surfers are
          <u>OF</u> the water... You surf because it feels
          good to be trimming down a wave, and
          being in harmony with nature. Not
          because you're trying to impress the girls
          or win a trophy.

Joe looks at Art as if he has just been initiated into an exclusive club.

                    JOE
          You're one of the special ones! "A Soul
          Surfer" ...

Art looks at Joe with admiration.

                    JOE
          Being a soul surfer bears responsibilities
          though. You're responsible for passing
          the history and tradition of surfing to the
          next generation, to keep the surf culture
          alive, to teach surfers how to live in
          peace with the ocean, and most
          importantly... to be a surfer of goodwill...
          You're the glue that keeps us all
          together... This is much more important
          than being on the surf team.

Art, feeling 10 feet tall, looks up at Joe.

                    ART
          A soul surfer, huh.

                    JOE
          I knew it was in you, the first time you
          walked into the shop...

Joe looks straight into Art's eyes

                    JOE
          Weezwe?

                    ART
               (smiles)
          Weezwe...

                                        DISSOLVE TO:

A PASSAGE OF TIME

Year 1983 - 5'11' NATURAL ART QUASAR. Quad fin design, swallowtail, with a neon curved stripe down the deck.

Year 1984 - 5'10" BYRNE. Thruster design, channel bottom deep "V", squash tail, sunset orange fade deck with red rails.

Year 1985 - 6'0" TOWN AND COUNTRY. Thruster design, squash tail, XL Yin & Yang logo on the nose, with smaller Yin & Yang logos on the deck, Full Blown Neon geometric shapes painted on the deck.

Year 1986 - 6'3" CHANNEL ISLANDS BLACK BEAUTY. Thruster design, rounded pin tail, all white deck with black outline on the rail.

Year 1987 - 6'6" RUSTY. Thruster design, pin tail, all white board with a single letter "R." on the deck. As minimalistic as it gets.

FADE TO:

1988

EXT. BEACH - SUNRISE (1988)

The sun is rising and Art is sitting at the picnic table by himself. He is checking out the 6-foot waves. Art is now 21, mature looking, physically fit, and a bowl cut hair style. His three-fin surfboard is leaning against the picnic table. The surfboard is completely white with the exception of a small logo that says Bajan Surfboards. Via walks up to the picnic table. Via is 21, mature looking, physically fit, and has a "New Wave" vibe about her. All the characters in this time period look like they have stepped out of a 1988 "Surfer Magazine".

Art and Via are now the local hotshots. Via lays her surfboard on top of the picnic table. Her 3-fin surfboard is the exact opposite of Art's. It is pasted with a multitude of sponsor's logos as well as the Bajan Surfboards Team logo. The difference in the 2 surfboards is significant. Art's board represents the "soul surfer" and Via's board represents the "contest surfer". Via is wearing a t-shirt that reads, "BAJAN SURF TEAM".

> VIA
>
> Hey Art. What's up?

> ART
>
> Oh, not much. Just getting ready for the
> morning session.

Via pulls out a brand-new bar of wax. She starts waxing her board in circular motions. Via is looking at the waves and occasionally looks at Art.

> VIA
>
> The waves look fun... Where've you
> been lately? I haven't seen you in the
> water.

                    ART
College has been killing me. It seems
like all I do is study and go to classes.
The only chance I get to surf is at
sunrise...

Art Looks around.

                    ART
I dig it though, 'cause I'm usually the
only one out...

Art longingly looks at Via.

                    ART
I miss those days when it was just you
and me... Surfing at sunrise... Our
Adventures... Being Friends Forever...

                    VIA
Those days are long gone. We're not kids
anymore, you know.

                    ART
Kids or not kids, I still miss those days...

                    VIA
          (rationalizing voice)
Look. I'm about to turn pro. Don't you
know how much dedication, effort, and
sacrifice that takes?

                    ART
I know...

> **VIA**
> There's no time to be playing children's
> games to see who can get to the beach
> first.

Art pauses and stares out into the ocean with introspection. He then looks up at Via.

> **ART**
> Well, we're both here this morning and
> that's all that matters...

Art looks at Via and smiles.

> **ART**
> I'm glad to see you Via.

Via looks at Art and smiles.

> **VIA**
> I'm happy to see you too Art...

Art and Via both reflect on the past.

> **VIA**
> Hey, are you going to the surf contest this
> weekend?

> **ART**
> I don't know... I don't think so...

> **VIA**
> Come on, it's only the biggest contest of
> the year. Even a soul surfer like yourself
> can watch a contest. It won't kill ya...
> There's surfers from 500 miles away
> coming. You can watch me beat them all.

ART
Alright, I'll be there... But in the
meantime, let's just get in the water, Miss
Pro Surfer.

Art and Via smile at each other, grab their surfboards, and head for the
water.

DISSOLVE TO:

SURF CONTEST

EXT. SURFING CONTEST – DAY

A SERIES OF SHOTS

A) A 1970's wood paneled Ford Country Squire station wagon with a surfboard on the roof racks pulls up to a crowded makeshift gravel and sand parking lot. It's full of cars and visiting surfers.

B) Devo, Ledge, and Tuna (shirtless) all get out the station wagon as if they are the center of the universe. Their surroundings and the other people around them are meaningless and inconsequential. Devo opens up the driver side door as Via puts on sunglasses and exits the car as if she is the prize fighter in the main event. Devo closes the door behind her and Via takes her surfboard off the racks. Via and her entourage have arrived!

C) FLASHFORWARD to Via surfing in the contest against other girls and dominating.

D) FLASHBACK to Tuna in front with Ledge and Devo flanked on each side. They plow their way through the crowd leaving a wide-open space for Via to walk in total freedom. The 4 of them in a cool swagger let everyone know that this is their beach, and they own it! Everyone and everything have to make way for Via! The surfer that no one can beat!

E) FLASHFORWARD to Via battling for position next to another girl in the surf contest and dropping into a wave.

F) FLASHBACK to the entourage walking past Joe and paying their respects.

G) FLASHFORWARD to Via shredding a wave.

H) FLASHBACK to Art cheering and hooting at the spectacle, as the entourage passes him and heads for the scaffolding that is covered with sponsors banners and flags.

DISSOLVE TO:

EXT. SURFING CONTEST BEACH - DAY

PRESENT TIME. A crowd of 300 people are on the beach. There are spectators, surfers who have entered the contest, groups of surfers who represent various regional surf teams, and entire surfing families rooting for their mother, father, sons, and daughters. Surfboards of various shapes and sizes are littered everywhere. It's the surfing event of the year and it's hopping!

Via and 5 male surfers are at the shoreline waiting for the horn to start their heat. The 6 surfers have different color, skin tight, Lycra jerseys on, and Via's is light blue. The horn sounds and 6 surfers go running in the water, jump on their surfboards, and feverishly paddle to the lineup.

                    COMMENTATOR (V.O.)
          Heat number 2 of the men's division is in
          the water. In the red jersey is Kanoa
          Aukai, in the green is Isaac Mirren, in
          yellow is Felipe Torres...

CUT TO:

Art is talking to BRUNA BRAGA. Bruna moved here from Portugal and she is part of the surf crew. In the FOREGROUND, the crowd is watching the surf contestants paddling out into the lineup.

                    COMMENTATOR (V.O.)
          In the dark blue is Ramzi Aziz, in orange
          is Jordy Richardson...

                    ART
          I think that's the best you've ever surfed.

                    BRUNA
I got super lucky. I out positioned the
other surfers in the heat and caught every
set wave. Everything just clicked...

                COMMENTATOR (V.O.)
Wait a minute! Did I say the men's heat!
Well hold onto your straw hats, because
in the light blue jersey is Via Franco!
She knows no boundaries, and has
entered the men's division! Dominating
the women's league is not enough for this
young champion. She's now taking on
the boys!

Art and Bruna turn their attention to Via and begin hooting and cheering
with the crowd.

EXT. OCEAN - DAY

ISAAC MIRREN in the green jersey and Via are side by side paddling for
position. Isaac and Via start exchanging words.

                    ISAAC
You don't belong here! This is the men's
heat. The MEN'S HEAT!

                    VIA
What... You can't handle that a girl might
just beat you.

                    ISAAC
Beat me? Don't get all emotional and
start crying when I humiliate you.

An oncoming wave approaches, Via and Isaac fight for position.

> COMMENTATOR (V.O.)
> Via Franco and Isaac Mirren are dueling
> it out for position. Oh! What a maneuver
> by Via Franco. That puts her into
> position. She's dropping into a nice
> wave. Via goes for her patented off-the
> lip slashback. Oooooh, digs a rail and
> wipes out. That's not gonna score well
> with the judges.

Via pops up to the surface and recovers her board.

> VIA
> (agitated)
> Aaaaagh!

Via looks up to watch Isaac in the FOREGROUND drop into the next wave right in front of her.

> COMMENTATOR (V.O.)
> Here comes a set wave. Isaac Mirren's
> on it. He's going for the cover up.
> Yeeew! What a tube ride. Right in front
> of Via. Oh! And what a spectacular off-
> the-lip! She can't be happy about that.

Isaac finishes his ride and paddles to Via.

> ISAAC
> Give it up! You belong with the other
> girls… On stage in the bikini contest...
> On second thought, don't bother. You
> couldn't even win that!

EXT. BEACH - DAY

The crowd on the beach are watching the competitors in the water.

COMMENTATOR (V.O.)
Stickers... Stickers... I see someone out
there with a handful of stickers.

All the grommets in the crowd shift their attention from watching the contest to finding out who has the stickers.

COMMENTATOR (V.O.)
Could it be John Marcucci?

John looks at the scaffolding and holds up his empty hands.

COMMENTATOR (V.O.)
How about Bruna Braga?

Bruna and Art look up to the scaffolding and start laughing. Bruna holds up her empty hands.

COMMENTATOR (V.O.)
Wait a minute... Who's that with his
hands full over there. Is that... No, it
couldn't be... It's... It's... DEVO!...
Get'em!

All the grommets spot Devo and rush towards him. Devo sees the onslaught of grommets coming after him and starts running. Everyone is laughing and giggling. Devo is throwing stickers in the air as the grommets chase him all around the beach. The crowd gets a big kick out of it and cheer for the grommets.

(NOTE: Devo's glasses have also changed. They now look like a type of modified swim goggle with extremely thick lenses. The goggles cover his entire eye sockets. They are one-of-a-kind glasses, very edgy, and very cool).

CUT TO:

Art and Bruna are standing next to each other talking.

COMMENTATOR (V.O.)

What an insane ride by Via Franco. She
needed that one desperately. She won't
win this heat, but with that ride she
should advance to the next round.

BRUNA

Why didn't you enter the contest?

ART

It's really not my scene.

BRUNA

But you're as good as anyone here. I still
don't understand why you didn't enter.

ART

I just don't think surfing is about who is
better than who. It's a competition
between yourself and the ocean... Not
against one another.

BRUNA

I don't see anything wrong with a little
friendly competition. It's part of human
nature.

CUT TO:

EXT. SHORELINE - DAY

The horn blows and the next heat of 6 surfers charge into the water while
Via and the other 5 surfers belly board to the beach.

CUT TO:

EXT. BEACH - DAY

Art and Bruna are still having the same conversation.

> ### ART
> Yea, we humans love to compete, you've got a point there. But for me, surfing is different. It's the visceral experience of sharing THE STOKE from a fellow surfer who's hooting and cheering you on for the wave you're riding. That energy gives you the drive to push the limits and become a better surfer. It's the exact opposite in competitions. It pits surfer against surfer, tensions become high, and tempers flare. It's no longer surfing in its purest form.

Via visibly upset, walks up to Art and Bruna.

> ### VIA
> That was one of the worst heats I've ever had. You cannot believe what the guy in the green jersey was saying to me.

> ### BRUNA
> Don't let it bother you. He was probably trying to psyche you out.

> ### VIA
> (angry)
> No, it was way more than that! This guy was being a total jerk!

> ### BRUNA
> Don't worry about it. I'm sure you advanced to the next round.

                    VIA
          Yeah... Yeah... Yeah...

                    ART
                 (lecturing)
          See this is what I'm talking about. The
          only person who is happy at a surf
          contest, is the person who comes in first
          place... The peaceful co-existence has
          been shattered.

Via gives Art a nasty look and throws her surfboard into the sand. Via
with outrage in her eyes, looks at Art.

                    VIA
          Peaceful co-existence! You have NO
          IDEA what just happened out there in the
          water... No idea at all!

Art becomes angry and upset.

                    ART
          See... This is why I didn't want to come!

                    VIA
          Didn't want to come. This is my dream!
          I've worked so hard to make it this far... a
          little support from my best friend might
          be nice... Maybe your problem is, you
          can't stomach watching me win... After
          all these years, you're still sore about not
          making the surf team when I did. Aren't
          you?

                    ART
          I'm not sore... Surfing is about having
          fun, that's all!

                    VIA
              (sarcastically)
          Yeah ok, Mr. Soul Surfer...

                    ART
              (sarcastically)
          Sure thing... Miss Pro Surfer...

Via walks away angry and heads to the scaffolding. Art is just as angry
and kicks the sand.

                                        DISSOLVE TO:

EXT. BEACH SHORELINE - DAY

Via is heading towards the shoreline where 5 other male surfers with
different colored jerseys are standing. She passes by Ledge and stops.

                    VIA
          Hey Ledge. Do you have any of that
          water proof eyeliner?

                    LEDGE
          Sure, Why?

                    VIA
          I want to look and feel like a fierce
          warrior! I want to wake the Quitu
          ancestors inside me!

Via looks at Ledge with unflinching determination. Ledge channels Via's
feelings.

                    LEDGE
          Oh Yeah! Now you're talking! I know
          just what to do... When those surfers
          look into your eyes, they'll turn to stone
          and sink to the bottom of the ocean.

Ledge draws a thick black line around her entire eyelid. Which gives her an edgy, punkish, take no prisoners look. Ledge looks Via squarely in the eyes.

LEDGE
Your Strength is unstoppable!!!

Via stands tall, grabs her surfboard, and confidently walks to the shoreline.

(NOTE: from now on, this will be Via's signature look whenever she is surfing in a contest!)

Via and the 5 male surfers are anxiously waiting for the horn to start the men's finals.

COMMENTATOR (V.O.)
This is what we've all been waiting for...
the men's finals! They're not too happy
with Via Franco in the mix... If anything,
I would say the men are looking a bit
nervous. But none the less, this is how
legends are born.

Via's attitude has changed dramatically. She stares at Isaac Mirren with a stone-cold look. It's as if she can see the future, and how the finals are going to end. It ends in total annihilation of the men surfers.

A SERIES OF SHOTS

A) The horn blows, they run, enter the water, and start sprint paddling through the waves to the lineup.

B) Isaac bumps Via on the paddle out to rattle her nerves. She is totally unfazed, and with a fierceness in her eyes, turns to the right, and paddles right over his legs and feet. Which actually startles Isaac.

C) Via jockeying for position, paddles around a surfer, catches the wave, and shreds the wave to perfection.

D) Isaac responds by catching a wave and riding it to perfection.

E) Via and Isaac are jostling for position. Isaac outmaneuvers Via. He is about to drop in, when a moment of hubris takes hold. He looks at Via and winks at her. This split-second delay causes him to misjudge the wave, hurling him into the air in a major wipeout.

F) Via drops into the next wave with complete confidence and sheer determination. She gets barreled, then does a bottom turn off the lip, heads back down the face of the wave where Isaac is paddling back out. She then does a roundhouse cutback sending a spray of water right into Isaac's face.

G) An aerial shot of all 6 surfers together. Via drops into another wave and surfs it as only a champion could.

H) Via is on the victory stand holding up the women's 1st place trophy and the men's 1st place trophy.

DISSOLVE TO:

SHEEP
SHUCKERS
INN

PARTY HOUSE

INT. BEACHHOUSE - NIGHT

A party of about 40 people is in the living room.   Everyone is dressed up in their best beach attire. The whole surf crew is there, Via, Art, Devo, Tuna, Ledge, Bruna, and other local surf personalities. It's a rich mix of ethnicities and races. There are surfboards and surf pictures hanging on the tongue-and-groove wooden walls. A live band, "The Ding Repair Men", are in the corner of the living room playing rockabilly surf tunes. A sign behind the band says, "CONGRATULATIONS VIA. WISHING YOU WELL, ON THE PRO TOUR"! Via is in front of a group of people using hands and arm movements to describe an earlier wave she rode. It's a party in full motion and grooving!

Art and Devo are at the kitchen bar which divides the living room and kitchen. There is a table full of various dishes of food and snacks. While Devo is talking, he is sifting through a bowl of blue tortilla chips, scrutinizing, and searching for the deformed triangle shapes that are folded over like a cylinder. These chips resemble perfectly shaped a-framed tubing waves.

> DEVO
> I can't take the crowds in the water
> anymore. I'm going to New Zealand...
> It's a surfer's paradise over there.

> ART
> Yeah, I hear ya'. There's countless point
> breaks...

Devo finds a waved shaped chip and delicately places it on a blue plate.

                    ART
And Raglan is one of the longest lefts in
the world.

                    DEVO
Dude! But the best part is... There's
nobody out at these places! No crowds,
no hassles... Just you and the surf,
surrounded by green mountains, and tons
and tons of sheep!... I'm goin' there! I'm
getting out of this rat race.

                    ART
I'm with you on that. You know where
I'm going! As soon as I graduate college,
I'm off to the Islands, where it's just me
and the waves!

                    DEVO
You should...

Art looks into the living room and establishes eye contact with ERIKA
SIMMONS. She is not dressed in the usual surf attire. You can tell she
did not grow up at the beach. She has an artistic, philosophical,
intellectual look and feel about her. For a brief moment their eyes lock
and they are both hypnotized by each other as if time has stopped. Art
does not hear a word Devo just said.

                    DEVO
Well, what do you think?

Art snaps out of it his trance with Erika.

                    ART
Huh... What?

DEVO
You know, about us going to New
Zealand and opening a bar called Sheep
Shuckers Inn.

ART
Oh yeah, right, uh...

DEVO
We could have sheep shearing contests,
and instead of lady's night, we could
have sheep night. All sheep get in free.

ART
(laughing)
Sounds killer, but nothing's stopping me
from going to the Islands!

Devo picks up a broccoli spear from an uncleaned plate. He sticks the broccoli spear upside down on the plate with the chips. A CLOSEUP of the plate reveals a diorama of a perfect beach scene. The blue plate represents the ocean, brown cheese dip is spread flat to represent sand, a series of 4 broccoli spears are turned upside down in the cheese dip representing palm trees, sour cream represents the whitewater, and finally 4 folded over blue tortilla chips are placed in the sour cream. It is a masterpiece of art! Depicting a perfect set of waves breaking at the beach.

Via walks up, looks at the diorama, and then at Devo. She is speechless, starts shaking her head, and smiles.

VIA
What's up Devo!

DEVO
Oh, not much. Just hanging out like a
hair on a biscuit.

Via quietly laughs about DEVO's comment. Meanwhile, Devo's attention is still focused on his diorama. Art looks at Via.

> ART
> Sorry if I blew your scene at the beach today. You just happened to walk into the middle of a conversation about why I don't surf contests.

Via's smile turns to aggravation.

> VIA
> Look... I was doing my best to win today. I came to you for support, and what do I get? More of your stupid granola eating, hippie philosophy about soul surfing.

> ART
> (defensive)
> What exactly does that mean?

> VIA
> (berating tone)
> You're as good as any surfer I know! No one CARES anymore about being in HARMONY with the ocean... All surfers care about now-a-days, is SHREDDING the wave as hard as they can.
> Competitive surfing and the pro circuit is the NEW WAVE... Get with the times...
> Soul surfing is dead!

Art and Via tensely stare at each other. Devo puts his arms around Art and Via and tries to break the conflict.

DEVO
Doo-Doo...

He looks both of them in their eyes.

DEVO
The opposite of Don't-Don't...

Devo's attempt to break the tension doesn't work. Art breaks free of Devo's arms.

ART
(angry and sarcastic)
Yeah. Well. Good luck with your pro
career!

Art quietly leaves the party and walks out the front door. SURFER #2 comes up and "high fives" Via.

SURFER #2
Congrats on joining the pro circuit.
We're gonna miss you.

Via watches Art leave and is not really paying attention to Surfer #2.

VIA
Thanks. I'm gonna miss you too and
everyone...

At the same time an OUT-OF-TOWNER and his buddies are looking at Devo and making fun of his glasses.

OUT-OF-TOWNER
Nice glasses, Aquaman.

> DEVO
>
> Geez... What's in the water today...
> Everyone's so uptight. Was there a sewer
> discharge in the ocean or something?

The Out-of-towner thinks Devo is talking about him. He approaches and knocks off Devo's glasses, which reveal a portion of his face that never sees the sun. His eye sockets and temples are completely white. Whereas the rest of his face has a dark tan. This tan line gives the effect of a white bandit mask or raccoon face.

> DEVO
>
> What's wrong with you Dude!

The Out-of-towner gets buffed up and ready to fight.

> OUT-OF-TOWNER
>
> Are you callin me Sewer Discharge!...
> Raccoon face!

Ledge walks up.

> LEDGE
>
> Why don't we all just take a breather and
> calm things down.

> OUT-OF-TOWNER
>
> First, Aquaman and now the Queen of the
> Seas shows up. What kinda party is this?
> A giant freak show!

Ledge becomes very upset and gives a death stare to the Out-of-towner. At that very moment, Tuna breaks into the melee, shirtless, and full of muscles. He approaches the Out-of-towner. Tuna with a rage in his eyes, stares down the Out-of-towner, grabs him by the collar, and starts shaking him back and forth violently.

TUNA
(with rage)
LISTEN HERE, SEA LICE!

Tuna looks Ledge square in the eyes.

TUNA
This is no freak show!

Tuna then looks at the Out-of-towner.

TUNA
If you're calling Ledge a freak! Then
you're calling me a freak! You're calling
all of us freaks!

The Out-of-towner says nothing...

TUNA
And nobody... And I mean NOBODY!!!
Messes with Devo's glasses! I suggest
you leave now, before someone loses
their eyesight.

GROMMET #3 under the protection of Tuna yells out.

GROMMET #3
Yeah, BEAT IT sea lice!

The Out-of-towner and his buddies sulk out of the party and leave.

Via walks over to console Ledge. Via straightens out the shoulder strap
on Ledge's sun dress in a loving tender way.

VIA
This world is full of jerks! Don't let him
bother you. You're the most beautiful
person I know.

Ledge smiles at Via and gives Via a big hug. Ledge regains composer, and addresses the crowd.

> LEDGE
> Let's lighten this party up. We're here to give a proper sendoff to Via and wish her well on the Pro Surfing Tour.

The crowd cheers.

> LEDGE
> Hey Devo, get up there and sing a song for us!

Devo is not in a joyful place. He puts his glasses back on and sadly shakes his head no.

> LEDGE
> We're not taking no for an answer. Come on Devo!

With his head down, Devo still does not respond. Ledge starts chanting.

> LEDGE
> Strobe light... Strobe light... Strobe light...

The crowd now starts chanting.

> CROWD
> Strobe light... Strobe light... Strobe light...

Devo lifts his head and a tiny part of his frown turns into a smile. The crowd starts to cheer as they are still chanting.

> CROWD
> Strobe light... Strobe light...

Devo snaps out of it and now has a full-blown smile. He grabs Via by the hand and heads to the stage. The crowd cheers! The band starts playing a slow instrumental love ballad as Devo and Via each grab a microphone for the duet.

DEVO
(soothing mellow voice)
This is a song for all the lovers...

Boom! The band instantly switches tempo from a slow love ballad to the up-tempo total danceable new wave song - "Strobe Light" by The B-52s. The crowd goes wild!

A SERIES OF SHOTS

A) The band begins to play.

B) Devo starts to sing and act out the lyrics. He is trying to woo Via into making love with him under the strobe light. Via stands on the stage acting bored and disinterested. She wants nothing of Devo's advances.

C) Devo now sings with energy that tonight we make love under the strobe light. Just at that moment! The lights go dark and STROBE LIGHTS START FLASHING!!!! Everyone at the party goes crazy and starts dancing under the pulsating strobe lights.

D) The strobe lights turn off and the lights come back on. Devo starts singing about all the places he wants to kiss Via. Via starts to act intrigued and becomes interested in his advances.

E) Via starts singing, I want to make love to you under the strobe light.

F) Again, the lights go dark and the STROBE LIGHTS START FLASHING!!!! The crowd is now dancing at an uncontrollable frenzy as the strobe lights keep pulsing.

CUT TO:

EXT. PARTY HOUSE - NIGHT

Art is walking down the street alone. It is quiet. The only exception is the muffled thumping noises coming from the band playing at the party house. In the BACKGROUND, you can see the strobe lights flashing out the windows as Art walks away.

CUT TO:

EXT. BEACH - NIGHT

It is dark and quiet at the beach. The only light is from the fishing pier shining down on the water.

The only noises are the waves crashing. Art sits alone on the beach cross-legged with his surfboard and wetsuit next to him in the darkness. He is in an introspective state, thinking about what was said at the party and how he and Via are taking different paths in life. The ocean is his warm blanket and helps soothe the sadness he feels. Art stands up and starts putting on his wetsuit. He picks up his surfboard and starts walking into the darkness of the ocean.

A SERIES OF SHOTS

A) Art paddles out a few feet away from the pier pilings as the light shines down on him. He duck dives the oncoming waves into the darkness.

B) Art sits on his surfboard looking up to the moon. He is bobbing up and down with the trough and crest of the swells.

C) A FULL SHOT of Art's silhouette dropping into a 6-foot wave. He does a bottom turn and trims down the face. Gaining speed, he roller coasters up and down, finishing with an off-the-lip.

D) Via is onstage at the party. Someone hands her both trophies she won earlier in the day. She holds up the trophies with a sense of hard-fought accomplishment as the crowd cheers.

E) Art rides another wave with the pier and lights in the BACKGROUND.

F) Via is shaking hands and hugging her fellow surfers as they leave the party. They are congratulating her and wishing her well on the Pro Tour.

G) Art is walking alone on the beach with his surf board under his arm. He disappears into the darkness.

DISSOLVE TO:

FINEST
CHOPPED
CLAMS
CHOWDER
FRED'S

THE DATE

INT. CHOWDER FRED'S - EVENING

Art is walking into Chowder Fred's, as Craig (Ledge's alter ego to a conforming society) is walking out. Art high fives Craig.

                    ART
          What's up Craig!

                    CRAIG
          Stoken!

Craig walks out the front door.

Chowder Fred's is a diner type restaurant with a casual atmosphere and a surfing theme. There are antique surfboards hanging from the ceiling and on the walls. There are also old classic black and white pictures of surfers riding longboards from the 50's and 60's. Art walks up to FRED SOLOMON and orders his meal. Fred is the owner. He is an older surfer in his 60's, burly and in good shape, yet weathered with leathery wrinkled skin from 60 years of frying in the sun. Your classic "Old Salt". On the front of his uniform is the Chowder Fred's logo which is in a form of skull and crossbones. The crossbones are surfboards and the skull is a cup of steamy clam chowder.   The restaurant is a reflection of Fred, weathered, worn, and welcoming.

Art is wearing a damp bathing suit, a T-shirt with the Bajan Surfboards logo on it, and leather flip flops. His hair is wet and his feet are sandy.

                    FRED
          Do you want this to go?

                    ART
          Yeah Fred, I'm gonna cruise on home.

FRED
That'll be $4.56

Art pulls out some wet money and hands it to Fred. Fred drapes the wet
dollar bills on a napkin holder to dry it off.

FRED
(bewildered)
Did you go surfing????

ART
Yeah.

Fred gets a crazed look on his face.

FRED
But there's no waves!... It's been flat!
Flat for over a month!

ART
I know! I'm going through withdrawals.
I JUST HAD TO GET IN THE WATER!

FRED
I haven't been in the water sooooo long.
How was it?

ART
Ankle to knee high mini peelers. It was
perfection. So glassy, it was like surfing
on butter!

FRED
I've got to catch some waves! I'm
starting to lose my gills! It's been that
long! I'm going friggin cuckoo!

                    ART
              (in despair)
          Yeah, there's no end in sight. It's a
          surfing drought!

                    FRED
              (over dramatically)
          The likes we've never seen before...

                    ART
          I didn't even care the waves were ankle
          high. It felt good to be in the water.

Fred gets the crazed look on his face again.

                    FRED
          Stop talking about it! Stop the insanity! I
          can't take it anymore! Stop it... Just stop
          it...

Fred still crazed and muttering gibberish walks away and heads into the
kitchen. Art sits down at a small table and waits for his order. A few
tables away is Erika Simmons serving food to a family. She has the same
Chowder Fred's shirt on. Art looks over to the table and recognizes Erika
from the party. At the same time Erika looks at Art and remembers him
from the party. As they look at each other, their eyes lock once again, she
sets a drink on the table and smiles at Art. Art smiles back. Erika walks
away from the table and heads to Art. As she walks by, she looks down
at Art's sandy feet and points.

                    ERIKA
          You've got some sand in your toes.

Art perplexed, looks down at his sandy feet and then looks back up at
Erika as she passes by.

                    ERIKA
                  (laughing)
                Made you look!

Art starts laughing and makes eye contact one more time as Erika walks
into the kitchen. Erika comes out of the kitchen with a to go order and
sits it on the counter. With a romantic smile, she looks at Art and signals
his order is ready. Art with a flirty smile, walks up to the counter. He
looks down at his feet, then at Erika.

                    ART
              I just wanted to apologize for my sandy
              feet. My name is Art, by the way.

                    ERIKA
              I'm Erika. It's nice meeting you.

Erika is reading the food order stapled to the paper bag.

                    ERIKA
                  (flirting)
                A beet burger!

                    ART
                  (flirting)
              What's wrong with a beet burger?

                    ERIKA
                  (flirting)
              Oh... I don't know. I pictured you more
              as a shark sandwich kinda guy.

                    ART
                  (flirting)
              Sharks and I... We have come to a
              mutual agreement.

Erika is laughing with quizzical look on her face.

ERIKA
An agreement?????

ART
(flirting)
Absolutely! I don't eat sharks... And
sharks don't eat me...

Erika just shakes her head and starts laughing. Art smiles at her and starts laughing. He feels the chemistry between them and musters up the confidence to ask her out.

ART
There's a reggae show Saturday night. I
was wondering if maybe you would like
to go?

ERIKA
(pleased)
Yeah... That sounds like fun.

Erika notices the people at one of her tables are ready to order, they are looking a bit antsy and impatient. She hurriedly writes her number down on a piece of paper and gives it to Art.

ERIKA
I've gotta go. Give me a call later tonight
and we can talk about it then.

Both of them are enamored, look at each other one last time, and part their ways.

DISSOLVE TO:

EXT. REGGAE BAND AT BEACH - NIGHT

A reggae band is playing outdoors at a beach front bar. The bar is called "Kon Tiki". There are tiki torches and wooden tikis decorating the stage.

The beach is the dance floor. About fifty people are dancing with no shoes on. The "who's - who" of the surfing community are all here; Devo, Bruna, Ledge, Tuna, Fred, and even Joe. They are dressed casually with shorts, T-shirts, sun dresses, etc.

Plus, there are many people with dreadlocks in attendance. It's a cultural mash of people from all over the world. Everyone is dancing to the reggae beat.

Erika and Art are dancing in the crowd. They dance their way to Devo. Devo is the only person not dancing to the reggae beat. He is doing the "surfer stomp" which is the stomping of the right leg twice, then stomping the left leg twice, along with broad shoulder movements. This makes Devo stick out of the crowd like a sore thumb. Erika looks at Devo in bewilderment as he stomps.

                    ART
          Hey Devo... I'd like you to meet
          somebody...

All three are still dancing as Art introduces Erika to Devo.

                    ART
          Devo this is Erika... Erika, this is Devo.
          He's a good friend of mine, as well as,
          one of the most stylish surfers in the
          water!

Devo still doing the surfer stomp, looks at her.

                    DEVO
          It's nice meeting you.

                    ERIKA
          It's nice meeting you too.

                    ART
          What? No dance partner?

> DEVO
> Nope... Tonight, I'm just a lonely
> octopus, in a stray pigeon world...

Erika looks at Art and starts laughing. Devo stomps away to another area of the dance floor. Art and Erika keep dancing and moving around the crowd. Art acknowledges the presence of other people he comes in contact with such as Bruna and Fred from the restaurant. Joe and his wife MOLLY MONTGOMERY come up from behind. Joe abruptly pushes his way in-between Art and Erika. He puts his arms around the both of them. He moves his head from side to side and looks at Art and then at Erika as if he is watching a tennis match.

> JOE
> Hmmmmmmm... What do we have here?

> ART
> Hey Joe, this is Erika.

> JOE
> (smiling)
> Aaaah... Love is such a beautiful thing!

Art starts to blush and is embarrassed, while Erika thinks it's funny.

> ART
> (coyly)
> What are you talking about????

Joe, with a cheshire cat grin, twists his head towards Art and looks him in the eyes.

> JOE
> Hmmmmmm!

Joe with the same Cheshire Cat grin, twists his head in the opposite direction and looks at Erika.

JOE
Hmmmmmm!

Molly sees the embarrassment and torture Joe is inflicting upon Art.

MOLLY
Hey Joe-Joe...If love is such a beautiful
thing, then leave the boy alone... and
come dance with your wife!

Joe smiles and rolls his eyes one last time, as he gives a final glance to Art and Erika. He removes his arms, slowly backs away, and with a big grin starts dancing with his wife. Molly has a big grin as well. You can tell Joe and Molly are deeply in love with each other.

ERIKA
I like your friends... a bit on the eccentric
side, but I like em'.

ART
Yeah, I'm with you on that one! I think it
has to do with surfing and growin up at
the beach.

ERIKA
The beach huh?... That makes some
sense. People here value things much
differently than where I'm from.
Everyone here is living life to the fullest,
they don't seem to worry about what car
they drive, or how their hair looks. It's a
different world onto its own, raw, and to
the core of life.

ART
It's the ocean... The ocean IS the great
equalizer.

ERIKA
What do you mean by that?

ART
The ocean doesn't care if you're rich or
poor, young or old... The ocean doesn't
care about the color of your skin, gender,
social status... The ocean has no
nationality!... It punishes and rewards
everyone equally. The ocean grounds
you, makes you humble, and teaches you
that the world and nature is much, much
bigger than yourself... Much bigger than
any one surfer... It's a connecting force!
The surf community you see in front of
you... It's the shared experience of the
ocean among us. That force is <u>THE
BOND BETWEEN SURFERS.</u>

Art continues talking and sees Ledge walking towards him. Ledge is
wearing white linen pants and a white linen halter top. Art looks at Ledge.

ART
It allows you to be free... Free to be you...
Right Ledge.

LEDGE
Absolutely!

Ledge gives Art a big hug, and Art hugs Ledge back. Art then looks across
the dance floor at Joe. The CAMERA FOCUSES in on Joe, who is
dancing with his wife and being surrounded by the people who mean the
most to him.

ART
Surfing's one of the few sports where the
older you are, the more respected you
become. The older surfers are our wise
elders... our royalty... our legends...

Right at that moment, the crowd erupts into applause, hoots, and cheers. Art and Erika turn their attention to what is going on. Up on stage a singer grabs the microphone.

A FULL BODY CLOSEUP shot of the singer reveals a Black Woman dressed from head to toe in the traditional colorful African dress. She is absolutely stunning and the crowd goes wild. She says the words.

REGGAE SINGER
Harambe!

The crowd goes wild again. The reggae band starts playing and she starts singing with the most beautiful, sweetest, melodic voice ever heard. Her voice is so powerful it melts all the hearts in the audience. She starts singing a rendition from the live version of Rita Marley's, "Harambe".

(Note: This song is to symbolize love, harmony, and world peace. It demonstrates the unity of races, cultures, ethnicities, and religions throughout the world. This is a call out to humanity, that if this small microcosm of a crowd can put aside their differences and become a "People of One", then "All the World's People Can Come Together as One". Humankind still has a chance! This is a very powerful song and a very powerful message. It is absolutely intoxicating and extremely romantic for everyone. Especially, for Art and Erika).

A SERIES OF SHOTS

A) A CLOSEUP SHOT of the vocalist singing the first verse of the song. Which talks about how the African people were scattered all around the earth. The people in power hoping they would disappear and waste away. But no matter how hard they tried, no matter what they said, the children would still sing Harambe!

B) The crowd dancing and listening to the song in peace and harmony.

C) A CLOSEUP SHOT of the vocalist singing the second verse of the song. Which talks about the colors of the rainbow being the same as the colors of our skin. All the colors are together in harmony, all sailing in the same boat (which is the earth), all going down the same stream. And the children are still singing Harambe!

D) The crowd is grooving and smiling to the song.

E) A CLOSEUP SHOT of the vocalist who begins to talk to the crowd. She is explaining what Harambe means.

> REGGAE SINGER
> Harambe means working together,
> pulling together, reaching out to each
> other, caring for one another, sharing
> with each other.

She starts to sing again.

> REGGAE SINGER
> I want to hear you say... HEY
> HARAMBE!

The crowd repeats the chant back to the singer.

> CROWD
> Hey Harambe.

                    REGGAE SINGER
          Hey Harambe.

F) A CLOSEUP SHOT of Art and Erika, caught up in the emotions of the
romantically charged song and the crowd, chanting, looking at each other,
and smiling romantically.

                    ART & ERIKA
          Hey Harambe.

                    REGGAE SINGER
          Let me hear you say.

A CLOSEUP SHOT of Bruna chanting.

                    BRUNA
          Hey Harambe.

                    REGGAE SINGER
          The African way.

A CLOSEUP SHOT of Joe and Molly chanting.

                    JOE & MOLLY
          Hey Harambe.

                    REGGAE SINGER
          The children say.

A CLOSEUP SHOT of Ledge chanting.

                    LEDGE
          Hey Harambe.

                    REGGAE SINGER
          Bob Marley say.

A CLOSEUP SHOT of Devo chanting.

> DEVO

Hey Harambe.

> REGGAE SINGER

Everyone say.

It's a complete lovefest. Art looks at Erika and takes her by the hand, as the crowd is still chanting.

> CROWD

Hey Harambe.

G) An AERIAL SHOT of Art and Erika winding through the crowd, leaving the dance floor, and heading to the beach at night.

EXT. BEACH - NIGHT

Art and Erika walk down the darkened beach. In the BACKGROUND, the band and crowd can still be seen and the music can be heard playing, just more muted and quieter. In the FOREGROUND is a bonfire on the beach with people huddled around it. Art and Erika are walking by the fire when a shirtless surfer interrupts them.

> SURFER #3

Artimus! Bro!

SURFER #3 looks at the huddled crowd of people and acknowledges Art's presence.

> SURFER #3

Look everybody! It's Artimus. He's
come to join the sacrifice!

A CLOSEUP of the bonfire reveals a burning surfboard in the middle of the flames. Erika looks at Art in an extremely confused and shocked manner.

                    ERIKA
          A sacrifice????

                    ART
          Yeah, a surf sacrifice. Whenever there's
          no waves for an extended period of time.
          Surfers become so desperate... They are
          willing to sacrifice a surfboard and other
          prized possessions such as bars of wax,
          old surfer mags, flip flops... you name
          it... It's an offering... In hopes of ending
          the flat spell.

Erika starts to chuckle at Art in disbelief.

                    ERIKA
          You're not serious?

                    ART
          Oh, we're very serious... Or maybe...
          It's just an excuse to have a party, and
          burn off some frustrations of no surf.

Art with a magical twinkle in his eyes, looks at Erika

                    ART
          Here's the funny thing... More often than
          not... The waves pick up after a surf
          sacrifice and the flat spell ends. So I say,
          ON WITH THE SACRIFICE!

The crowd begins to cheer and hoot! Erika cracks up laughing, and right
at that moment Surfer #3 interrupts.

                    SURFER #3
          Hey Artimus! We need your underwear
          to appease the wave gods. It's the only
          way the surf will pick up!

                    ART
               (laughing)
          Can't help you. I haven't worn
          underwear in at least 5 years.

                    SURFER #3
          Dude! Contribute something... Or we're
          revoking your Surfing License!

Just then, Erika gets a giant smile on her face, looks at Surfer #3, and then looks at Art. She discretely slips off her underwear from beneath her dress and throws it into the fire. The whole crowd erupts into cheers and hoots. Art proudly looks at Erika, smiles, and starts hooting.

                    SURFER #3
          Yes! We're going to get waves for
          sure!!!!

The crowd shakes Erika's hand and pats Art on the shoulder. Art and Erika leave the bonfire and head towards the quietness of the sand dunes.

EXT. SAND DUNES - NIGHT

Art and Erika are sitting on top of a sand dune, looking at the ocean. The moon's reflection is glimmering off the surface.

                    ERIKA
          That's the craziest thing I've ever done in
          my life. I think the ocean is having an
          effect on me.

                    ART
That's the spirit!

Art and Erika are having a good time re-living the moment that just happened.

                    ART
So, do you go to college here?

                    ERIKA
Yeah, this is my first year... How did you know?

                    ART
I've seen you around campus a few times. And from the first time I saw you, I wanted to meet you.

                    ERIKA
That's too funny, 'cause I've seen you around also... What's your major?

                    ART
Business.

                    ERIKA
                 (surprised)
Business! I would have picked you for a Marine Biology Major.

                    ART
                 (laughs)
Everyone thinks that. I create quite a spectacle walking into a finance class sun burnt, wet hair, and flip flops.

                    ERIKA
Why business?

                    ART
Because one day, I want to own a surf
shop. I want to be just like Joe...

                    ERIKA
What year are you?

                    ART
I'm a junior... 2 more years... and I'm off
to the islands!

                    ERIKA
The islands?

                    ART
Yes! Ever since I started surfing, it's
been an obsession of mine to find out just
how big of a wave I can surf. That's
where some of the largest waves in the
world break. The islands are calling me...
Calling me in a way that I MUST go...

Art snaps out of his feelings of grandeur and focuses back on Erika.

                    ART
What about you. What's your major?

                    ERIKA
Marine Biology.

It's Art's turn to look surprised. Erika starts laughing.

ERIKA

Got you! Actually, my major is Architecture. From a little kid, I've always wanted to design buildings. I get so immersed in structures that touch the sky and are in sync with their surroundings. I view architecture as an art form.

ART

An art form? A building?

ERIKA

Absolutely! Buildings are mirrors of society that reflect the great achievements of that time period.   Here's a classic example. What pops into your head when I say ancient Greece?

ART

I think of mythical stone buildings with giant towering columns. The places where Greek gods lived.

ERIKA

Exactly! Is that architecture or is that art?

ART

Hmmmmmm...

ERIKA

I'm going to create buildings of wonder!
I'm going to sculpt structures that reflect
the zeitgeist of THIS very moment, in
THIS very time we are living in! The
landscape is my canvas!

ART

And the ocean is my canvas.

ERIKA

We are very similar, you and me. We're
just painting with different brushes...

Art holds Erika's hand and they look at each other as if they are kindred
spirits.

ERIKA

What's the world gonna do with us?

ART

2 crazy dreamers.

They both laugh. Art embraces Erika and kisses her. After they have
kissed, Art looks up to the stars.

ART

What a beautiful night.

Erika gazes at Art who is still looking at the stars.

ERIKA

A beautiful night, indeed.

DISSOLVE TO:

INTERMISSION

<u>SURFERS WANTED!</u>

-Calling All Surfers! Calling All Friends of Surfers!

-I Need Your Help

-Each and Every One of You Can Make a Difference

-We Have the Power to Come Together and Make This Movie

-This Will Be a Movie About Surfers, Made By Surfers, Financed By Surfers

-When You Contribute to the Film, You Become Part of the Film

-Take Pride in Saying, "I Helped Make This Movie! I Helped Make This Film a Reality!"

-Be a Part of the Movement

-Be a Part of the Movie

-Be a Part of Surf Culture

-Spread the Word

-Your Help Gets Me One Step Closer to Making This into a Feature Length Film

-THANK YOU!

www.tbbsurf.com

POWER TO THE SURFERS!

LET'S MAKE A MOVIE!

-First There Was "THE ENDLESS SUMMER"

-Second Came "BIG WEDNESDAY"

-Now "THE BOND BETWEEN SURFERS"

-An Authentic Movie About Surfing and Surfers

-A Grand Experiment, 25 Million Surfers Strong

-A Surfing Grass Roots Movement

-I Need Each and Every Surfer and Friends of Surfers to Make this Happen

-Your Purchases Will Go Towards Raising Money to Make the Film

WAYS TO CONTRIBUTE

1. Spread the Word to All Surfers and Friends of Surfers

2. Make It Go Viral!

3. Buy the Book (Amazon)

4. Buy the E-Book (Amazon)

5. Buy the Audio Book (Amazon)

6. Listen to the Audio Episodes (Podcast)

7. Buy a T-shirt (Online)

8. Contribute to My Crowdfunding Page

- For More Information Go To My Website www.tbbsurf.com or Scan the QR Code

-THANK YOU!

LET'S GET THIS MOVIE MADE!

REPTILE BROTHERS

EXT. OCEAN - DAY

The waves are waist to chest high and peeling perfectly. Bruna and a few other surfers are sitting in the lineup. They are all on shortboards. Art and Devo paddle up on old beat-up longboards that are relics from the 1960's. Devo has a cowboy holster and toy guns on his hip. (NOTE: Devo still wears the modified swim goggles with extremely thick lenses even while surfing). All the surfers are playing and joking around.

> SURFER #4
> Well, if it isn't "Longboard Larry" and
> "Amazing Mike". Didn't you guys see
> the sign on the beach? No tankers
> allowed.

Devo in his best Clint Eastwood impression.

> DEVO
> The party's over boys... You might as
> well paddle in. You don't stand a chance
> when we break out the reptile boards.

> SURFER #4
> What? That's ridiculous.

Devo pulls out the toy guns.

> DEVO
> (psycho voice)
> We will shoot anybody who gets in our
> way.

> SURFER #4
> That's ridiculous.

DEVO
(psycho voice)
Is it? Just watch us. There is no escaping
the wrath of the reptile brothers!

ART
Longboards rule!

BRUNA
We'll see about that.

It's on! Longboarders versus shortboarders, the rivalry begins.

A SERIES OF SHOTS

A) Devo drops in on Surfer #4. Devo shows his classic longboard skills. He stylishly cross-steps to the nose of the board, hangs ten, arches his back in a perfect curve, and raises an arm in the air.

While on the nose, Devo sees Ledge paddling out. Devo pulls his guns out of the holster and starts shooting at Ledge. He then blows on the tip of his guns like they did in wild west. Ledge's face has a very perplexed look. Ledge cannot compute what has just happened, and continues paddling out.

B) Art drops in on the next wave. He rides the longboard in classic 1960's fashion with style and grace. He cross-steps to the nose of the surfboard, crouches down, stretches out one leg, and does a cheater 5. He stands back up and cross-steps to the tail of the board. The wave pitches out, Art does a head dip, and finishes by kicking out of the wave.

C) Devo drops into a wave fin first. The longboard does a complete 180-degree spin. Devo regains his balance, trims down the wave, and does a 360-degree spin with his body. He cross steps up to the nose and finishes his ride with a "Quasimodo".

D) Devo drops in on another surfer. The surfer wipes out. Bruna has had enough of Devo and Art's shenanigans. She drops in on Devo making him nose dive into the water. Art see's this and now it's his turn to drop in on Bruna. Bruna and Art start dueling it out. They trade positions on the wave trying to make the other fall. They are both laughing and giggling. Bruna wins and makes Art wipeout. She raises her arms in victory and shouts.

                    BRUNA
          GIRLS RULE!

                                        CUT TO:

A CLOSEUP of Art's surfboard washing up on the beach all by itself.

Art swims in and retrieves the longboard. He sees Erika in the water and paddles towards her. She grabs onto the surfboard.

                    ART
          Nothing beats a good longboard session.

                    ERIKA
          I never realized how different
          longboarding is compared to
          shortboarding... I love all the tricks you
          do.

                    ART
          Yca, thcrc's no better feeling than
          trimming down the wave on a longboard.
          My goal is to surf exactly like they did in
          the 50's and 60's. So, if someone from
          that era took a time machine to the
          present, and they saw me riding this old
          log. They'd say, "Yep... nothing's
          changed after all these years".

Art notices Erika looking at the board.

                    ART
          Do you want to give it a shot?

                   ERIKA
          What? Go surfing?

                    ART
          Sure, why not. It's easier on a longboard.

Erika looks apprehensive.

                    ART
          Come on... It's a nice calm day out there.

Erika's apprehension turns into a smile of excitement, which infects Art's
face in the same fashion.

                   ERIKA
          Ok.

                    ART
          Alright! Let's go.

Erika is clumsily paddling the board while Art helps her through the small
breakers. Art is standing in about waist to chest high water holding onto
the surfboard. Erika is trying to sit on the board and keep her balance, but
she keeps falling off. They are both laughing.

A waist high wave approaches. Art grabs a hold of the board while Erika
is lying on it.

                    ART
          Paddle, paddle, paddle!

Erika begins paddling. Art pushes the longboard as the wave approaches.
Erika and the longboard take off. She rides it on her belly for a while then
begins to stand up and shakily rides the wave for a few seconds.

ERIKA

Whooo!... Yeeew!... I'm surfing!... I'm
surfing.

ART (O.S.)

Yeah! Go... Go...

ERIKA

Yeeeew!... Whooo!

She finally loses her balance and falls, disappearing into the whitewater.

CUT TO:

Art and Erika are in the water holding onto the longboard. Art is on one
side and Erika is on the other side. They are looking at each other face to
face.

ERIKA

I can't believe I was actually surfing.

ART

Yeah, you did it.

ERIKA

What an unbelievable feeling. I can see
why you love surfing so much.

They both gaze into each other's eyes and smile.

DISSOLVE TO:

ROMANCE AT SUNSET

EXT. WATERWAY - SUNSET

A small jon boat is motoring down the waterway. Old beach houses on stilts surround both sides of the bank. The sun is setting and the wind is still, creating a mirror image reflection of the beach houses onto the water.

EXT. DOCK - SUNSET

The jon boat approaches a dock. As it gets closer, the image becomes clear that it is Art. He is carrying flowers in one hand and steering the boat with the other hand. Erika is eagerly awaiting Art's arrival. Art pulls up to the dock. A look of love and a smile breaks out on his face. He ties the boat off and steps out with flowers in hand.

                    ART
          Along the way, I picked you these
          flowers.

Erika takes the flowers from Art's hand.

                    ERIKA
          Oh, they're beautiful.

Erika embraces Art and gives him a kiss. There is a loving aura in the air. After the kiss, Erika and Art walk down the dock to her house which leads to the porch. There is some outdoor furniture, a hammock, and a dinner table set up for two.

                    ERIKA
          I thought since it's going to be such a
          beautiful night, we could eat outside.

ART
Sounds killer to me.

ERIKA
(jokingly)
Yeah, nothing's better than a can of beans
out on the porch.

ART
I'm deeply touched. No one's ever gone
to such great lengths for me before.

As they walk down the dock, Art and Erika are laughing. Art puts his arm
around Erika.

CUT TO:

EXT. PORCH - NIGHT

Erika has cooked a gourmet dinner for Art. They are eating by candlelight
out on the deck.

ART
I remember seeing you at the party,
thinking nothing in the world could be
more beautiful than you.

ERIKA
I thought the same thing. I was hoping
we were going to bump into each other,
but you mysteriously disappeared.

ART
I had some thinking to do. Changes in
life… Sometimes, are a tough pill to
swallow.

Art pauses and reflects on those changes.

                    ART
          So, I went surfing.

                  ERIKA
          In the middle of the night?

                    ART
          I just needed to get in the water. I do
          some of my best thinking sitting in the
          ocean and feeling the pulses of life. I'm
          at peace when I'm surfing.

                  ERIKA
          I totally understand. I have places like
          that too. Places that clear my head.

                    ART
          Where?

Erika fixates on her hands as they start forming curves in the air.

                  ERIKA
          I have this fascination with curved lines.
          I know a building that has the most
          beautiful curves I've ever seen. The way
          it silhouettes on the skyline is
          breathtaking. It fits seamlessly within the
          surroundings, as if it was meant to be
          there. It overwhelms me, to the point I
          lose track of time and space...

                    ART
          It almost sounds like you are describing a
          wave.

ERIKA
Yes, I can see the similarities...

Erika has an epiphanic moment and drops her hands hard on the table.

ERIKA
(excitedly)
OH MY GOSH! THAT'S IT!

ART
(startled)
What????

ERIKA
I can use waves as a source of inspiration
in my architecture! The curves... The
horizon... The reflection of light... I can
see it! It's all right here... It's all right in
front of me!

Art holds Erika's hand.

ART
You are amazing!

They both gaze into each other's eyes as the candlelight reflects off their faces.

DISSOLVE TO:

EXT. BEACH - DAY

Art, Devo, Bruna, and a few other surfers are hanging around the picnic table. Some of the surfers are sitting on the table while others are standing. There are surfboards strewn everywhere.

BRUNA
I got a phone call from Via last night.
She won the Bells Beach contest in
Australia!

The group of surfers all becoming excited and cheer. The exception is Art who sits silently staring out into the ocean.

GROUP OF SURFERS
Stoked... Killer... Yeew...

BRUNA
(excitedly)
She beat out Freida Zamba in the finals,
on what was said to be one of the best
heats of the season, if not of all time.
They were battling it out, matching each
other wave for wave. Freida would drop
into a wave and totally annihilate it like
no one has seen before. That is... until
Via would drop into the next wave and
match her move for move. One wave the
judges gave Freida a perfect score, only
to have Via follow up with a perfect
score. The heat was so close and intense,
no one could tell who won. After the
score sheets were added up, Via won by a
single point.

DEVO
Yeew, local girl turned surf hero!

                    BRUNA
With only two more contests to go in the
season, she has broken into the top 10
and has a strong hold on 8th place.
Everyone's saying she's gonna get rookie
of the year!

                    DEVO
                  (proudly)
And just think, we all grew up surfing
with her.

Devo "high fives" a fellow surfer, and everyone is feeling proud. Art still
sits quietly, staring out to the ocean.

                                        DISSOLVE TO:

<u>A PASSAGE OF TIME</u>

A) Art and Joe are at "The Cape" looking at 10-foot waves peeling off the river mouth.

B) Via is at the pro surfer's season-end banquet. She is holding up a big trophy that says rookie of the year. The audience is applauding and cameras are flashing.

C) Erika is showing Art a beautiful building with curves in it. She is using hand gestures and pointing to the sky.

D) Art and Erika are laying in the grass, holding hands, and looking at the curved building.

E) Art is surfing a 6-foot wave with no one out in the water.

F) Via is surfing a 6-foot wave in a contest.

G) Erika is showing a college architect project. The building model has curves that resemble waves and swells.

H) Art and Erika are sitting on surfboards in the water. It is dark. They are looking up to the full moon and stars.

I) Via has reached celebrity status, and is signing autographs at a surf shop. One of the kids hands her a "Surfer Magazine" with her picture on the cover. A caption reads "Via Franco Clinches World Title in her 2nd Year on the Tour". Via reflects on the picture, smiles proudly, and signs it.

J) Art is dressed up in a black gown and cap. He is holding up his college diploma in one arm, and the other arm is around Erika. In the BACKGROUND is a huge banner that says, "CLASS OF 1990".

FADE TO:

1990

THE WAVE HOUSE

THE WAVE HOUSE

INT. ERIKA'S LIVING ROOM - DAY

Art and Erika are sitting on a couch holding hands. In the other corner of the room, are some travel bags stuffed tightly with clothes and surfboards wrapped in a board bag. It is a very solemn atmosphere in the house. They are both trying to put the event that is about to transpire in the back of their minds.

> ERIKA
> Ever since we first got together, I knew
> this day was gonna come. It just seemed
> like 2 years was too far away to worry
> about, and here it is... The day you move
> to the islands.

Erika embraces Art.

> ERIKA
> I don't want you to go.

A tear runs down her cheek.

> ART
> You've made me the happiest guy on the
> earth, I love you so much, and nothing
> makes me feel sadder than leaving you.
> But I made a promise to myself that I
> would not stay back for any reason.

Art with an unwavering look of determination on his face.

                    ART
I just have this fear... If I compromise on
my dream, it's gonna lead to
compromising other things in my life.
Next thing you know, I'll be fifty years
old, living inland, with a big beer gut
watching a football game on TV, and
remembering when I used to surf... To
me, that's my worst nightmare.

                    ERIKA
I know... But it still doesn't stop the ache
in my heart.

                    ART
I'm going to miss you so much.

Art embraces Erika. Erika reaches over the couch and picks up an
architectural model of a miniature house in the shape of a wave. The
miniature house is very small and fits in the palm of her hand. She gives
it to Art.

                    ERIKA
I made this for you. It's your perfect
little beach house.

                    ART
It's beautiful! It's OUR little beach
house. Maybe one day, you can build it
and we can live there.

                    ERIKA
              (sobbing)
I would love that.

Art and Erika hug again. It's a despairing moment for both of them. Erika
breaks free from the long embrace.

> ERIKA
> (sobbing)
> It's time... We've got to go to the airport.

DISSOLVE TO:

INT. CAR - DAY

Erika is driving Art to the airport. It is a very sad time for both of them. Neither one is talking. Art is coming to the realization that he is leaving behind the place he grew up, his friends, his family, and the girl he loves. He is taking it hard.

Erika drives to the beach for a final goodbye to the waves. They get out of the car and walk to the beach. Joe, Devo, Ledge, and Tuna are all hanging out at the picnic table waiting for him. Art gets a bit choked up and tries to smile.

Ledge walks up to Art and hands him a fashion illustration. It's a colored sketch of Via, Art, Joe, Devo, Tuna, and Ledge all hanging out on the beach with their surfboards.

> LEDGE
> This is so you don't forget about us...

Art takes the illustration, looks at it, and gets choked up.

> ART
> It's all of my friends... Ledge, it's a
> masterpiece...

> LEDGE
> Every surfer dreams of moving to the
> islands... Few have the <u>Guts</u> to do it.
> You're making it happen! We're all so
> proud.

Art looks at everyone with tears down his face.

                    ART
You're the best friends that anyone could
have... It's not gonna be the same without
you...

Art walks over with his arms wide open and corrals everyone together in
a giant group hug. Everyone has tears coming down their faces.

                                        DISSOLVE TO:

INT. PLANE - DAY

Art looks out the airplane window. All he can see is miles and miles of
blue ocean. He turns back in his seat and continues to write a letter on the
food tray in front of him. The miniature wave house is also on the food
tray. A NARRATION of the letter takes place.

                    ART (V.O. NARRATION)
Dear Erika,
As I sit in this plane, it all of a sudden
hits me that I'm headed for a strange land
that I've never been before, and I'm
leaving behind someone I dearly love. It
puts a very hollow feeling in my stomach
as I get closer and closer to my
destination. As I face the overwhelming
challenge ahead of me, I say to myself,
"What am I doing here? It's just going to
be me, my bags, and my surfboards. Will
I be able to make new friends? Will the
local surfers accept me? Will I be able to
find a place to live, or even get a job?
What about the friends I've left behind?
My family? My sense of being? And
<u>Especially You</u>.
                    (MORE)

(CONTINUED)

ART (V.O. NARRATION)
Will I just be another fading memory,
slowly to be forgotten?" All of this
because I have to find out what my
limitations are in the surf and in the
ocean. My whole life I've dreamed about
it... Today it's coming true. All I know is
my heart feels empty and is aching for
you, and I think to myself... IS IT
WORTH IT?

CAPTAIN (V.O.)
The plane will be landing in
approximately 15 minutes. The weather
is partly cloudy and 78 degrees. I hope
you have enjoyed your flight on Moutere
Airlines.

ART (V.O. NARRATION)
I Love You… Art

DISSOLVE TO:

EXT. AIRPORT - DAY

Art's plane lands on the tarmac.

A SERIES OF SHOTS

A) Art is strapping his surfboards on top of the rental car. There are palm trees and tropical foliage in the background.

B) Art is heading down a two-lane road. The ocean is on the right side, and the green tropical mountains are on the left side.

C) Art is standing at the edge of a vertical cliff that is about 200 feet above sea level. From this vantage point, he has a 180-degree view of the jungle-like cliff that leads directly to the clear blue ocean. To the right is a black lava rock point which also ends at the ocean. The crystal-clear water is dotted with brown coral reefs which are sharply contrasted with the white sandbars that lie in-between to them. A little further offshore the waves are breaking perfectly over the reef. The waves have 6-to-10-foot faces, and there are about 5 people out. Art is watching them surf.

D) Art with a surfboard under his arm, is walking down a shady trail on the very steep cliff. The cliff has been totally overrun by tropical vegetation which blocks out any view of the sky or the ocean. Occasionally, there will be a small opening in the densely green vegetation that brings in a ray of sunlight and view of the blue ocean below. The trail becomes steeper and man-made steps are carved into the trail. Art carefully walks down the steps until he reaches a spot where the cliff goes completely vertical. A rope is attached to a tree that dangles over the side. He grabs the rope, turns around, precariously balances himself with a surfboard under his arm, and descends down the rope. At the bottom, the trail subsides to a flatter grade.

Art is walking along the shady trail as it leads out to the sun lit beach. He puts his surfboard down underneath a shade tree, takes his shirt off, darts to the beach, straps his leash on, and paddles out to the lineup. The water is so clear, all the intricacies of the reef can be seen underneath him as he paddles.

E) Art is sitting on his surfboard in the lineup. He's taking in the whole scenery. In the FOREGROUND, he sees the sea level perspective of the cliff and the black lava rocks. The waves have 8–10-foot crystal clear faces and breaking left. A set approaches and he catches his first wave in the islands.

He drops in on a 10-footer and screams down to the bottom setting up for a backside off-the-lip. He does the off-the-lip, drives down the face, does another backside off-the-lip, and pulls out of the wave.

Art starts paddling back out to the lineup with an extremely stoked expression on his face as a local Polynesian girl drops in on a wave in the FOREGROUND. She rides the wave with style and grace.

F) An AERIAL SHOT of Art surfing a wave to perfection. It shows the colors of the clear blue water, the black lava rocks, and the green tropical cliffs.

DISSOLVE TO:

Art is sitting at the lineup. 2 local Polynesian surfers are mumbling in Pigeon English. They are looking and laughing at Art. Art has a look of complete happiness as he absorbs his new magical surroundings. He has no idea they are talking to him. LOCAL #1 stares Art down.

LOCAL #1

Ey' hoale!

Art does not hear him. He is still in his state of utter joy.

LOCAL #1

Ey' hoale! I'm talking to you.

Art hears him this time and snaps out of his nirvana.

LOCAL #1

Either go inside, or go outside... But get
outta' my face!

The 2 local surfers start laughing at Art, not quite knowing what to do, Art smiles and paddles further outside. A set of waves come in and the 2 local surfers scurry to catch them. The local surfers each catch a wave and completely annihilate it. From Art's perspective, he sees the back of the wave where the local surfers are appearing and disappearing each time they do an off-the-lip. Another local surfer, KIMO PAKALA, paddles up to Art.

> KIMO
>
> Ey' don't worry about them bruddah's.
> Just stay outta' the way, an you'll be fine.

> ART
>
> Thanks.

> KIMO
>
> No worries, brah.

Another set of waves come in and Kimo takes off on the first one and fires down the line. Art takes off on the second one and follows suit.

EXT. BEACH - DAY

Art walks up to the shade tree where his clothes are, and sets his surfboard down on an exposed root. Kimo is sitting nearby. Art walks over to Kimo.

> ART
> (with humility)
> I hope you guys can handle another surfer
> on the island.

> KIMO
>
> Ey' brah... There's always room for a
> good surfer like you.

Kimo extends his hand and Art shakes it.

> KIMO
>
> My name is Kimo.

> ART
>
> Glad to meet you. I'm Art.

                    KIMO
You did the right thing by not causing a
ruckus with those two Mokes. 'Cause
they pound hoales heads and eat them for
breakfast.

                    ART
Yeah, I've heard stories about guys like
that.

                    KIMO
Believe every one of those stories and
don't forget em'. Ey', but don't think
we're all like that. Most of us are filled
with plenty of Aloha... How long are you
visiting?

                    ART
I got here a few days ago, and I'm
planning on living here permanently.

                    KIMO
Welcome. You found a place to live?

                    ART
No.

                    KIMO
A good friend of mine needs a roommate.
I give you the number.

                    ART
Thanks.

                    KIMO
        Ey', there's also a bulletin board next to
        the grocery store. There's all sorts of ads
        for getting jobs, cars, and surfboards. If
        it's for sale, it's on that board.

                    ART
        Cool.

Kimo gets a stick and writes the telephone number and the name Aiko in
the sand. He picks up his surfboard, walks to the path, and disappears
into the jungle.

                                    DISSOLVE TO:

AIKO
CUSTOM
SURF
DESIGNS

AIKO

EXT. HOUSE - DAY

Art walks up to the front door of a house that has the typical Polynesian architecture. There are banana plants and papaya trees in the front yard. Art knocks on the door, but no one answers. He waits for a second and knocks again. Still no answer. As he heads to the car, he notices a figure at the end of a cliff point sitting down with a surfboard. Art looks at her and starts walking to the point.

EXT. CLIFF POINT - DAY

AIKO MATSUDA is sitting crossed legged with her surfboard on her lap. Aiko is Japanese. She wears her hair in a braid. She is one of the premiere shapers of big wave surfboards on the island. She is sitting at the end of the cliff point on a plot of green grass. Aiko is sanding one of the fins on her surfboard. The cliff point is about 30 feet wide and drops vertically 250 feet straight down. Both sides of the cliff have small "U" shaped coves filled with crystal clear water and coral reefs. Art walks up to Aiko. Art is checking out the unbelievable view as Aiko sits there sanding away. Aiko is sanding and looking at her surfboard. She knows Art is next to her but has not looked up at him yet.

> AIKO
> Killer view, ey'!

> ART
> Unbelievable... I've never seen anything
> like it.

Art looks around some more then looks down at Aiko

ART
What's that you're doing?

Aiko looks up at Art.

AIKO
There's not enough foil in the fins... see.

Aiko lifts the board up and points to an outside edge of the fin. Art crunches down to take a look.

AIKO
Fins are one of the most important
components of a surfboard, but one of the
least understood… You can have the best
shaped surfboard, put a set of crappy fins
on it, and that board'll ride like a dog.

ART
Huh, I never thought about that.

AIKO
Most surfers haven't.

ART
What size board is that?

AIKO
It's a 9'10' rhino chaser. I shaped it for
the upcoming big wave season.

Aiko hands him the tail of the surfboard, and Art picks it up and begins to scrutinize it.

AIKO
This board'll catch waves you don't want
to get into.

                    ART
          I believe that!

                    AIKO
          See the rails?

Art flips the board on its side and looks and feels the rails.

                    AIKO
          They're a bit thicker. It breaks over a
          quarter mile out and the wind tends to
          chop the face up. The chop will bounce
          off the rails. Plus, you need lots of
          length since the wave is so relentless and
          fast. When it's 30-foot faces, you've got
          to get speed to make the 20-yard close-
          out sections... or die.

Art gives her a bit of an astonished look, then looks back at the board.

                    ART
          I would think a board made for massive
          waves like that would have a thicker
          stringer.

                    AIKO
          No, 'cause at a certain point you want the
          board to snap in half.

                    ART
          What???

AIKO

That's right snap... A perfect example is this one guy who was surfing 35-foot waves. He was making a bottom turn as the lip of the wave crashed down on him. The power of the wave smashed him on his board and broke his leg in half near his hip. As he surfaced, the last thing he remembered was his foot hitting him on the side of his head... The guy almost drowned... Now, if his board would've snapped in-half on impact, the whole situation would've never happened.

Art hands the surfboard back to Aiko.

ART

Do you think you can shape me one of these?

AIKO

I don't shape boards for just anybody... Especially, boards made for waves of this magnitude. When you're talking about surfing giant waves, you're talking a special breed of person. That person is not necessarily the best shredder on the beach. Instead, that person has the determination to drop in on a huge wave, look death straight in the eyes, and CHARGE IT! It's not made for someone who comes over here for a month just to say they've surfed the islands.

                    ART
Well, I'm planning to stay here
permanently. In fact, I'm looking for a
someone named Aiko who lives in that
house over there.

Art points at the house he just left.

                    AIKO
Oh, you must be Art, right?

                    ART
That's right.

                    AIKO
Well, it's nice to meet you, I'm Aiko.

Aiko shakes Art's hand.

                    AIKO
Kimo said you're a pretty good surfer,
and that you give off a good vibe. Kimo
is a well-respected surfer and a great
judge of character, so if you want the
room, it's yours.

                    ART
Cool, I'll take it... Since Kimo has given
me such an outstanding reference, does
that mean you'll shape me a rhino chaser
like this?

Aiko looks up at Art with a CHUCKLE AND GRIN

                    AIKO
Nope, not 'til you prove to me, you've
got what it takes.

ART
Well then you better start working on it,
'cause I know I've got it.

They both look at each other and laugh.

DISSOLVE TO:

AIKO
AIKO

THE BOARD

INT. KITCHEN - MORNING

Art is eating a bowl of cereal at a small kitchen table. Beside him is a window that looks out to the ocean. There are huge swells stacked to the horizon. Aiko walks into the kitchen.

> AIKO
>
> Are you ready?

> ART
>
> Yeah, where are we surfing?...

Art looks out the window at the swells lining up like corduroy to the horizon.

> ART
>
> The swell's cookin!

Art shoves the last 3 bites of cereal in his mouth, gets up from the table, and throws the bowl in the sink.

> ART
> (talking with his mouth full)
> Let me grab my board and we're outta'
> here.

> AIKO
>
> Forget about the board. You don't need it.

> ART
>
> What do you mean, I don't need it? It's firing!

                    AIKO
          We've got all day to surf. Right now
          there's more important things to do.

Art looks at Aiko in disbelief.

                    ART
          What?... After all the times you've told
          me to blow off this and blow off that to
          go surfing, and now when the waves are
          cookin, there's more important things to
          do?!

                    AIKO
                (with a grin)
          Yep.

Art begins to mutter to himself as he follows Aiko out the door.

                    ART
                (muttering)
          The first big swell of the season, and she
          says there's more important things to do.
          I had to make friends with a bunch of
          surfers who have their priorities all mixed
          up. All I've heard for the last 7 months
          is, this is the islands, and surfing always
          comes first.

Aiko with a smirk on her face, pops Art in the back of the head sending
hair flying in all directions, as they walk out the front door.

                    AIKO
          Quit your whining and get in the car.

                              ART
          I'm telling you, the priorities are all
          screwed up. Not going surfing...

EXT. MOUNTAIN TRAIL - DAY

Art, Aiko, and Kimo are walking up a very steep trail. There is green
tropical foliage everywhere. The trail runs up the middle of a ridge with
only about 10 feet separating either side of the steep mountain.

                              KIMO
          We're almost there... Right around this
          corner.

A clearing in the foliage produces a magnificent view. They are at an
elevation of about 1,500 feet. The view is one of Mountainous jungle,
square tracts of taro fields, and a giant "U" shaped bay. Inside the bay are
patches of whitewater. Art, Aiko, and Kimo look out and instantly
become mesmerized.

                              KIMO
          Ah, here it is... This is the spot where
          you can see the wave work all of its
          magic.

                              ART
          Unreal.

Aiko points to the right-hand side of the bay.

                              AIKO
          See that section of whitewater at the tip?

                              ART
          Yeah,

AIKO
That's where the wave starts when it's
big and peels for 200 yards. See that
calm area where no whitewater is
breaking on the left-hand side.

Art strains to find it by looking deeply into the horizon.

ART
Yeah, I see it.

AIKO
That's the safest place to paddle out. It's
a very deep channel and never breaks in
there. Plus, you can watch the wave peel
right in front of you, see how big the sets
are, devise your game plan on where your
gonna lineup, and how your gonna surf it.

KIMO
It's at least 20 feet out there.

AIKO
And 20 feet is about a 40-foot face.
When it's that huge, you always have to
watch out for any 25-foot rogue waves.
At 25 feet a giant wall of whitewater will
break all the way across the mile-wide
mouth of the bay. Devouring anything in
its path… Including you.

KIMO
The wave is a fast freight train right.
When it gets sizeable you have to watch
out for the 20-yard closeout sections. If
you see a closeout section approaching...

Kimo describes how to maneuver the wave with his hands.

> KIMO
> You need to make a quick bottom turn, travel up to the top of the wave, and rocket down the face just in front of the lip. At this point you will be free falling, but you will be traveling at the same speed as the lip. It's the only way to make the section. If you don't do that, the wave will smash you to pieces.

> AIKO
> The only other advice we can give you is don't drop in on anyone, don't ditch your board unless everyone else ditches their boards first. And finally, if you ever start to paddle for a wave, never, and I mean ever! Chicken out. It's better to go over the falls on a 20-foot macker, snap your board to pieces, break your leash, black out from almost drowning, and have some grommet save your life, than it is to pull out of the wave. The only way to gain respect on the island is to CHARGE IT! Now, if you promise me to do what I just told you, and go out every time, no matter how big it gets, or how scared you are, or how close to death you may feel... 'cause you will feel that way... I'll shape you that rhino chaser you want.

Art with a serious face, looks at Aiko and Kimo

                    ART
          I promise.

Art shakes Aiko's hand and Kimo puts his hand on top of theirs.

                    AIKO
          Alright then. You got yourself a board.

                                        DISSOLVE TO:

IF ZIGGY STARDUST WAS A SURFER
BAJAN SURFBOARDS
LEDGE

FINGER TO THE MAN

EXT. CITY SCAPE - DAY

Via in her paneled station wagon with a surfboard on the roof racks is driving down a city street with skyscrapers on each side. The station wagon pulls into a covered parking garage under a very tall building. Via gets out of the car, walks to the elevator, gets in, presses a button, and heads up.

INT. UPSCALE ARTSY OFFICE - DAY

Via enters the office which reveals a wide-open space. Its décor is super hip and super artsy. She walks up to the front desk, checks in, and is escorted by a hipster looking model. There are models, dressed in Haute Couture fashion of the early 90's, walking and hanging around. Via looks at the models in confused astonishment. The models look at her the same way. They are sizing Via up and even sneering at her total lack of fashion. Via is feeling like a fish out of water.

A fashion photo shoot is happening as she walks past them. She is led to an office. The model opens the door, lets Via in, and closes the door.

INT. OFFICE - DAY

COLTON HALL is an older man who is trying to look much younger and hipper than he actually is. He is sitting behind a desk. Plastered all over the walls are pictures of him with fashion models by his side.

> COLTON

Ah, Via. Come in, have a seat. I'm glad
to finally meet you. The phone is so
impersonal.

Via sits down on a plush leather couch. Colton comes from around the desk and sits next to her.

> COLTON

Congratulations on the world title. I've
been following your surfing career... I
just want to say you're so beautiful out
there surfing. Bikinis just love your
body.

> VIA
> (perplexed look)

Thanks?

> COLTON

And that eyeliner!... You're WHITE
HOT! Everyone wants to look like you.
To look like a surfer. This is why I
contacted you. I'm developing a new
line of surf clothing, and I want you to be
the face of the new brand!

> VIA
> (excitedly)

Really! That sounds very cool.

> COLTON
> (pretentiously)

What I create, is more than cool. My
clothing designs have influence all
around the world!

Colton puts his hand on her knee.

                COLTON
I'm going to make you a STAR!

Via moves her leg away from his hand.

                COLTON
You will be seen everywhere, on the
covers of fashion magazines, TV
interviews, and commercials. We will
make appearances at all the international
runways, New York, Milan, London,
Paris!

                VIA
What about the surfing tour? How am I
going to do both?

                COLTON
The schedule's intense. You'll probably
have to miss 2 or 3 surf contests.

                VIA
2 or 3 contests! I can't win The World
Title, if I miss those contests. You don't
understand, this is what I've worked hard
for my entire life.

                COLTON
Sacrifices have to be made. You don't
understand (demeaning her) I'm going to
make you a Superstar! An Icon! You'll
make more money than you ever will
surfing in <u>Those Contests</u>. In fact, I'm
going to offer you a MULTI-MILLION-
DOLLAR CONTRACT!

Colton puts his hand on her knee again. Via abruptly moves her leg and is getting a bit uncomfortable.

                    VIA
Have you ever surfed?

                    COLTON
No. What's that got to do with anything.
I set the trends... I set the fashion. If I
say the "surfer look is in", the fashion
world follows. You'll be in every
department store in the nation. This line
of clothes is going to make you famous...

                    VIA
Well, being a surfer has a lot to do with
it. You don't know anything about
surfers, about the sport, you don't know
anything about me, or what that eyeliner
symbolizes... I'm just a girl in a bikini to
you.

                    COLTON
You know, there's plenty of girls out
there that would do anything, I mean
anything to have a million-dollar contract
with me... Colton Hall.

He puts his hand on her knee and moves it gently up her thigh.

                    COLTON
          You need to grow up. Nobody throws
          away a million dollars. This is how the
          industry works, honey. There's strings
          attached to everything. Especially, multi-
          million-dollar contracts. Certain perks I
          get to enjoy, a way for you, to thank me,
          if you know what I mean. It's part of the
          deal.

Colton's hand goes further up her thigh and he tries to kiss her. Via becomes enraged and throws his hand off of her leg.

                    VIA
          Listen here you creep! Screw your
          clothesline and screw your million
          dollars! ALL I WANT TO DO IS
          SURF!

She jumps up and flips a coffee table over. Colton is startled, even scared, he jumps up, and cowardly backs into the corner. Via is seen yelling at him and moving her arms erratically.

Via storms out of the office still yelling at Colton. All of the commotion disrupts the photo shoot. The models are looking at her with confusion and horror. She looks at them in pity. Via can be seen talking to the models, pointing into the office, and making gestures that Colton is a scumbag.

In the BACKGROUND is one female model in the corner smiling uncontrollably. The model realizes that "Colton the Creep" has finally gotten what he has deserved...

A SERIES OF SHOTS

A)   The paneled station wagon driving down the city streets with skyscrapers on each side.

B) The paneled station wagon in a rural setting heading back home to the beach.

C) The paneled station wagon driving past Bajan Surf Shop and parking at the beach.

D) Via is sitting on the picnic table looking at the waves, alone, and talking to herself.

E) Ledge walks up, sits next to Via who is crying, and consoles her. Ledge is listening to Via's troubles. Via's body language tells the whole story of what just happened.

F) Via is crying and Ledge gives her a big hug.

G) CLOSEUP of Ledge hugging Via. Tears and makeup are running down Ledge's face as Ledge can relate, better than anyone, to the pain Via is feeling. Ledge does not wish this kind of pain for anyone and cries for Via's injustice.

DISSOLVE TO:

SPECIAL GUEST

EXT. PLUMERIA TREES - DAY

Art is in a green field next to 3 plumeria trees that are completely covered in flowers. He is reaching up, picking flowers, and placing them in a bag.

EXT. CLIFF POINT - DAY

Art is sitting in the green patch of grass at the end of the cliff point. He is stringing a lei with the flowers he had just picked and looking to the ocean.

CUT TO:

INT. AIRPORT - DAY

Art is looking out a glass window as an airplane taxies up to the gate.

CUT TO:

Art is watching the passengers walking out of the hallway. He's eagerly awaiting the person he has come to meet. In the middle of the crowd, Erika appears. They both get big smiles, rush towards each other, and embrace.

> ERIKA
> Oh Art, it's so good to see you.

> ART
> I thought this day would never come

They embrace each other again, then Art breaks away from her. He reaches into a bag and pulls out the lei he made on the cliff and puts it around her neck.

                              ART
                    Welcome to the islands.

Art kisses her.

                             ERIKA
                   These flowers are beautiful...

She brings the flowers to her face and smells them.

                             ERIKA
                   They smell absolutely divine. You know
                   I'm putty in your hands when you give
                   me flowers.

                              ART
                   Good, 'cause we've got 2 years to make
                   up for.

Caught up in the moment, they both stare at each other, smiling, and not
saying a word. Erika snaps out of the blissful trance.

                             ERIKA
                   Oh yeah, I got some stuff here from Joe.

Erika reaches into her handbag.

                             ERIKA
                   Joe said you might need these being on a
                   desolate island and all.

Erika pulls out a bathing suit and hands it to Art. Art holds them up and
looks at them.

                              ART
                   Baggies! Stoked! Mine are so dry rotted.

Erika pulls out 2 T-shirts with the Bajan Surfboards logo on it.

                    ERIKA
And he said, these are so you don't forget
about us at home.

                    ART
Killer!

Erika looks a little deeper in the handbag and pulls out a few more items.
The first of which is a couple of leashes.

                    ERIKA
And here's a few more things he said
would come in handy. Let's see, how did
he say it...

                    ERIKA
              (imitating Joe's voice)
Here's a couple of leashes, 'cause I know
he's snapped more than one.

                    ART
And I have.

Erika puts the leashes back in the bag, and pulls out a handful of wax,

                    ERIKA
              (imitating Joe's voice)
Give him all this wax, so he'll quit
bumming it off of everybody at the
beach.

                    ART
              (laughing)
I do no such thing.

She puts the wax back into the bag, and pulls out 3 Velcro watchbands
each being a different color.

ERIKA
(imitating Joe's voice)
Give'em these Velcro watchbands, 'cause
I know the one he's got on his wrist is
about to fall off.

Art looks down to his watchband which is old, faded, and tattered.

ART
Hmm... He's right.

Erika puts the watchbands back into the bag. She fishes around and pulls out a key chain with the Bajan Surfboards logo on it and a key attached to it.

ERIKA
And finally, this.

ART
A key?

ERIKA
He wouldn't give me an explanation. He
just told me to give it to you.

ART
That's odd.

ERIKA
Maybe it's a key to a buried treasure
chest.

ART
Or better yet, maybe it's a key to your
heart.

                    ERIKA
          I don't think so. It's gonna take a bigger
          key than that to unlock this heart.

They both start laughing. Erika puts the baggies and T-shirt back in the
handbag.

                    ART
          Let's get outta' here. There's so much I
          want to show you.

Art picks up the handbag. Excited, Erika hugs Art and kisses him on the
cheek.

                    ERIKA
          I can't wait.

                                        DISSOLVE TO:

EXT. CLIFF POINT - SUNSET

Art and Erika are walking to the edge of the cliff point behind the house
at sunset. They arrive at the grassy patch at the end of the cliff and sit
down.

                    ART
          Well, what do you think of the island so
          far?

                    ERIKA
          It's wonderful. I never thought there
          could be so much beauty on one small
          island.

                    ART
          You haven't seen nothing yet. Just wait
          'til you see the places I'm gonna take you
          to. I thought for starters we could go
          down to this cove tomorrow...

Art points down to the "U" shaped cove. He becomes a little more excited and starts giving detailed descriptions with his hands as he looks down to the cove.

                    ART
          The tide's gonna be so low that the tops
          of the coral reefs will be sticking out of
          the water and you...

Captivated by Art, Erika sits there smiling at him not paying attention to the cove or the hand descriptions. Instead, she just gazes at Art who is clueless to her enchantment.

                    ART
          Can actually walk on them. The cool part
          is, there'll be tidal pools full of tropical
          fish. One time I even found an octopus.
          We can go shell collecting...

Erika smiling, leans over, starts kissing him, and begins to interrupt his explanation.

                    ART
          But if the creature is still inside the shell,
          you'll have to throw it back. Then there's
          ah... ah...

Art begins to stutter and stammer, he turns his head, and looks at Erika who is smiling and giggling. Her joyfulness is contagious and he starts smiling and giggling with her. Then they both begin to kiss.

DISSOLVE TO:

A SERIES OF SHOTS

A) Art and Erika are snorkeling in the clear blue water. They are surrounded by coral reefs and tropical fish.

B) They are hiking to a 1,000-foot waterfall. At the base of the waterfall is a giant pool. Art and Erika holding hands, jump in the water, and go for a swim.

C) They are having a romantic dinner at an open-air restaurant that overlooks the mountainous cliffs plunging into the ocean. The sun is setting with brilliant gold, green, and blue colors colliding with one another.

D) Art cuts down a stalk of bananas in the jungle. He carries the bananas in one arm, and his other arm is around Erika.

E) In a red and white VW bus, they are driving down a deep red clay road, juxtaposed by bright green sugar cane fields surrounding them on all sides.

DISSOLVE TO:

EXT. LAVA ROCKS - DAY

Art and Erika are walking on a slab of black lava rocks. On one side are vertical green cliffs. On the other side is the crystal blue ocean. They are heading to a saltwater pond that has been trapped by the lava rocks.

EXT. LAVA POND - DAY

They are both standing next to the lava pond which is adjacent to the ocean. Art is on a rock and strips down to his bathing suit. He pulls out of a bag two pairs of swim goggles and hands one to Erika.

> ART
> Here, put these on.

> ERIKA
> Swim goggles? What for?

Erika in bewilderment watches Art put the goggles on his head and fits them to his eyes. He looks goofy with them on, but at the same time sexy. He looks at Erika.

> ART
> Trust me, just put em' on.

> ERIKA
> Ok?

Erika begins to strip down to her bikini. Art adjusts his swim goggles one last time, steps on a rock at the edge of the pond, and in a meditative state dives in.

INT. UNDERWATER - DAY

He sails through the water as if he is flying, and bubbles are coming off his body. Art comes to the surface, takes another breath, and goes underwater. He watches Erika dive in, as she glides through the saltwater pond.

ERIKA'S POV - UNDERWATER

Erika encounters a multitude of colorful tropical fish that have been trapped in the pond. She swims underwater looking at all the fish and algae covered lava rocks.

EXT. SURFACE - DAY

Erika comes up for a breath and is totally amazed. She looks over to Art.

> ERIKA
> I've never seen anything more beautiful
> in my life... Each spot you take me to, is
> prettier than the last. You've been a
> wonderful tour guide these past few
> weeks.

> ART
> Well, I figured I would save the best spot
> for last.

Art dives underwater, swims by a bunch of tropical fish, and up to Erika. He surfaces, takes a breath of air, takes off his goggles, and embraces Erika. Erika takes her goggles off and embraces Art.

> ART
> I've never seen you more beautiful than
> you are right now... I love you so much.

> ERIKA
> I love you too.

They look into each other's eyes and begin to kiss. The kiss turns passionate. All of a sudden, while they are kissing, Erika begins to cry. She stops kissing, continues crying, and hugs Art.

ART
What's the matter?

ERIKA
(crying)
I'm gonna miss you so much... I've just
started getting used to living my life
without you, then I come here for 2
weeks and it's like we were never apart.
And tomorrow, I'll be back on the plane,
alone, and without you. It's as if you've
died and all I'm left with is your
memories. It took me a year to get over
the first time you died in my life, and
now, I'm going to have to do it all over
again. It hurts so much. I can't keep
doing this.

Erika gets out of the water and Art follows. Erika wraps a towel around
her and Art dries off and puts his shirt on.

ERIKA
When are you going to live a normal life,
leave this place, stop surfing, come back
home, and get a real job? It's time to
grow up, make something of yourself.

Erika looks at Art in an exciting yet pleading manor.

ERIKA
We can do it together, make a life
together!

ART
What you call normal, I see as claustrophobic. Commuting an hour to work, stuck in an office, clocking in and clocking out, never seeing the light of the day. Repeat, repeat, repeat - day after day - year after year - decade after decade. It's a never-ending treadmill...

Art looks at Erika in an exciting yet pleading manor.

ART
Once you graduate, stay here with me! I can show you what's normal. We can have a beautiful life right here! I know we can. I've seen it. I can show you families that have done it... We can build a life here and live in the wave house!

Erika lets go of Art's hand and sits on a lava rock.

ERIKA
What would I do here? Architecture is my calling, my passion. I want to build buildings, build cultural institutions, build centers of art for people to immerse themselves in. I would rot here.

ART
(sad)
And I would rot in your world...

Art looks out to the ocean in a deep sad gaze.

ART
All I want to do is surf...

> ERIKA
> This is our Achilles heel... Neither one of
> us are willing to compromise...

Erika looks into Art's eyes with deep sadness.

> ERIKA
> Our passions... our dreams... are stronger
> than our love.

Art puts his head down in sadness.

> ART
> We'll always be painting with different
> brushes.

DISSOLVE TO:

EXT. CLIFF - DAY

Art is sitting on a cliff near the airport looking out into the ocean. He has a sad look on his face. As he is sitting there, a plane flies overhead. Art looks up to the plane.

INT. PLANE - DAY

Erika with a somber look, stares out the window. She sees the coastline and a figure of a person sitting on a cliff. She can tell it is Art. Erika gradually watches the figure disappear as the plane flies further and further into the ocean.

EXT. CLIFF - DAY

With a tear running down his cheek, Art gazes out into the ocean as the plane slowly disappears on the horizon.

DISSOLVE TO:

A PASSAGE OF TIME

Year 1992 - 8'6" BRIAN BULKLEY. Hawaiian big wave gun, tri fin, pin tail, all white deck.

Year 1993 - 9'6" DICK BREWER. Hawaiian big wave rhino chaser, single fin, triple stringer, all red deck with a Dick Brewer Lei Logo.

Year 1994 - 9'0" JEFF BUSHMAN. Hawaiian big wave Sunset Beach gun, tri fin, pin tail, red rails, and a yellow deck.

FADE TO:

1995

ROYAL
PACIFIC
SURFING
INVITATIONAL
AIKO

THE ROYAL PACIFIC

INT. SURFBOARD SHAPING SHACK - DAY

CLOSEUP of a small artificial Christmas tree with what appears to be snow falling on it. There is a strange sanding noise in the BACKGROUND. The camera PANS OUT from the Christmas tree revealing a shaping shack. The shack has rough cut foam surfboard blanks stacked in the corner and iconic pictures of famous female surfers on the walls. Aiko is wearing a mask that filters out the dust. Her body and face are covered in white foam dust which contrasts beautifully with her black hair. Aiko is shaping a surfboard on a wooden stand. She lifts her mask up and blows the white dust off the surfboard, which floats onto the Christmas tree.

Art enters through the door, puts on a mask, and walks over to Aiko. Aiko is still shaping away with a look of concentration on her face. Art starts eyeing the board over.

> ART
> You've outdone yourself on this one.
> Who are you shaping it for?

Aiko still shaping away.

> AIKO
> It's for Via Franco. She's gonna be
> surfing in the Royal Pacific, and she
> wants me to shape her a big wave board.

> ART
> I know you're stoked on that.

                    AIKO
          Shaping a board for Via Franco! You
          better believe it!

Aiko quits shaping, slides her face mask up to her forehead, and looks at
Art. Art does the same thing with his face mask.

                    AIKO
          Didn't she come from the same town as
          you?

                    ART
          Yeah, we grew up surfing together. We
          were best friends, like two peas in a pod.

                    AIKO
          I didn't know that... How come you
          never said anything about her?

Art with a look of emptiness and hurt stares at the Christmas tree.

                    ART
          I don't want to talk about it.

                    AIKO
          Don't want to talk about it! She's your
          best friend!   When was the last time you
          talked to her?

                    ART
                (somber tone)
          About 6 years ago, just before she turned
          pro. We had a falling out... And we
          haven't seen each other since.

> AIKO
> (irritated)
> 6 years! Are you kidding me! The both
> of you should be ashamed of yourselves!

Art looks down in shame.

> AIKO
> We have a saying in Japan... "Walking
> with a friend in the dark is better than
> walking alone in the light".

Aiko puts her dust mask back on, pushes Art away in disappointment, and continues shaping.

DISSOLVE TO:

EXT. TROPICAL BEACH - DAY

A large crowd has gathered at the beach. A scaffolding has been erected with a banner that says, "ROYAL PACIFIC SURFING INVITATIONAL".

EXT. SCAFFOLDING - DAY

A "Wide World of Sports", SPORTSCASTER is talking into a camera next the scaffolding. His yellow sports jacket and tie do not fit the island scene. The juxtaposition is plainly evident that he is completely out of place in the surfing world.

> SPORTSCASTER
> Welcome to the Royal Pacific Surfing
> Invitational. This is one of the most
> prestigious women's events in surfing.
> Surfers covet this championship almost
> as much as the world title itself. Why...
> Because it proves who's the best big
> wave surfer.

PUALANI HAUKEA and KEONE AKAMAI, with their hair wet and surfboards under their arms, walk by. A crowd of onlookers are following them.

> SPORTSCASTER
> And here are 2 of the favorites, Pualani
> Haukea and Keone Akamai. The
> Hawaiians dominate this event, and those
> women will be tough to beat.

Via walks out of the water with Aiko's surfboard under her arm. The surfboard has Aiko's signature koi fish painted on the deck. She gets mobbed by the fans.

> SPORTSCASTER
> One of the few surfers who has a chance,
> is 5-time World Champ, Via Franco! She
> has come close, but has never won the
> coveted Royal Pacific. Let's get a quick
> word from her.

The sportscaster walks over to Via. Via, dripping wet, is signing autographs from a swarm of people around her. He muscles his way in and begins the interview as she continues to sign autographs.

SPORTSCASTER
It looked like you were getting some
solid rides out there. How do you feel
going into the finals?

VIA
In the past years I haven't done so hot in
this event. It takes a while to learn how
to surf the power and the size of these
waves. To prepare myself, I focused the
entire year surfing the big wave spots of
Todos Santos in Mexico, Pico Alto in
Peru, Mavericks in Northern California,
and of course, I logged quite a bit of time
in Hawaii. Plus, I was lucky enough to
get a board shaped by Aiko Matsuda who
lives in the outer islands. She's one of
the prominent big wave shapers of our
time.

SPORTSCASTER
It sounds like you're prepared this
season.

VIA
All I can say is... nobody's gonna take off
deeper, drop in steeper, pull in longer,
wipe-out bigger, or charge it harder than
myself! And when the Hawaiians realize
this, you better strap on your seatbelts
and enjoy the ride, 'cause you're never
gonna see so many surfers going for
broke.

Via walks away from the sportscaster. The mob of people follow her still trying to get autographs.

> SPORTSCASTER
> There's no doubt about it, Via has come to win! Stay tuned, because The Wide World of Sports will be right here giving you all the action.

A SERIES OF SHOTS

A) Via, the 2 Hawaiian girls, and 3 other female surfers run into the water with surfboards in hand. They sprint paddle out to the breaking waves. They all have different colored jerseys on.

B) Via drops into a 15-foot face, does a sweeping bottom turn, heads for the inside section, and gets a stand-up tube ride.

C) Pualani drops into a wave and surfs it to perfection!

D) Via and Keone see an oncoming wave and maneuver for position. They are so close to each other that they are bumping rails and elbowing each other. Keone is also surfing on one of Aiko's boards.

Keone gets position and drops into a huge tubing wave. She makes it out of the barrel and rides the wave flawlessly.

E) Via takes off on a huge wave and rides it with grace and style. She finishes the wave and paddles to the beach.

F) Via reaches the beach and becomes mobbed by her fans. She is dripping wet and signing autographs once again.

G) Via, elated, is on the stage holding up a giant trophy that says "Royal Pacific Surfing Championship". The other surfers are congratulating her.

> DISSOLVE TO:

REUNIFICATION

EXT. HOUSE - DAY

Art pulls up to the house in his VW bus, gets out with his waiter uniform on, walks through the front yard, and opens the front door.

INT. LIVING ROOM - DAY

Via and Aiko are sitting in the living room talking to each other. They look up as Art enters. Art and Via both have a stunned and surprised look on their faces.

> ART
>
> Ho man, Via, what's happenen.

> VIA
>
> Oh... Oh... not much. After winning the
> Royal Pacific, Aiko invited me over to
> the outer islands for a little "R & R".

Art, with a smirk on his face, shifts his eyes over to Aiko. Aiko returns the glance with a placated look on her face.

> ART
>
> Aiko, this is all your doing isn't it.

> AIKO
> (smiling coyly)
> What... What are you talking about????

Art pauses for a moment. It's uncomfortably quiet. Both Via and Aiko stare at Art waiting for him to say something. Art looks at the both of them and cracks a smile.

> ART
>
> It's really good seeing you Via.

The tension eases and all three have big smiles. Art goes over to hug Via.

> ART
>
> What a perfect time to show up! I'm sure
> you've heard, the biggest waves of the
> season are about to hit.

> VIA
>
> Yeah, Aiko's been telling me all about it.

> ART
>
> It's a Primo Swell... And there's no better
> person I'd rather be surfing with… Than
> you...

Art and Via smile at each other.

> VIA
>
> Same goes for me...

DISSOLVE TO:

INT. ART'S BEDROOM - BEFORE DAYBREAK - DARK

Art is lying in bed. He slowly wakes up and looks at the illuminated clock which reads 4:47 AM. Art rolls over and turns the light on. He stretches and groggily gets out of bed. He picks up a pair of baggies that are on the floor and puts them on. A t-shirt is lying on top of the dresser. As he picks up the T-shirt, about 5 unopened letters and the miniature wave house are uncovered. He puts on the T-shirt and picks up the 5 letters. They are all addressed to Erika, and they all are stamped, "RETURN TO SENDER". Art flips through the letters and lets out a big sigh. He puts the letters down and walks over to a window. He stares out the window listening to the waves crashing. Art takes in a deep breath of fresh air and walks out of the room.

INT. LIVING ROOM - BEFORE DAYBREAK - DARK

Art walks into the dark living room.

                    ART
          Wake up you...

Art flicks on the light. He only sees a blanket and a pillow on a pullout couch. Art realizes he's been had. Via got up earlier than him! He now has a defeated look on his face.

                    ART
          Lazeeeey... bum... Dang it!

Art starts looking for Via and does not find her in the house. He walks outside and sees Via in the dark putting her surfboard in the back of Art's bus. A huge grin comes upon Via's face when she sees Art. Art with the look of a beaten puppy shakes his head.

                    VIA
               (facetiously)
          Oh, don't mind me, I was just loading up
          the surfboards. I hope I didn't wake you.

                    ART
               (defeated)
          No, you didn't.

                    VIA
               (facetiously)
          I thought you island guys got up early?...
          What was I thinking? I guess it's true
          what they say about island time,
          nobody's in a hurry.

> ART
> (laughing defensively)
> You know how it is when you catch
> waves of this quality all the time. You
> can afford to sleep in.

Art and Via Smile at each other and start to laugh. Via puts her arm around Art.

> VIA
> Let's go surfing.

EXT. BEACH - SUNRISE

As the sun rises, Art and Via are standing at the shoreline watching the huge 25-to-30-foot waves break. Via and Art are both standing with their surfboards Aiko made for them. Art puts his surfboard under his arm and looks at Via. Via puts her surfboard under her arm and looks at Art. They both look at each other like gladiators ready for battle, dive in the water with their surfboards, and begin paddling to the lineup. In the RIGHT-HAND FOREGROUND, they watch huge 25-to-30-foot waves perfectly peeling. PAN OUT to an AERIAL SHOT of them paddling out and the big waves breaking in front of them on the horizon.

A SERIES OF SHOTS

A) Art makes a huge drop, does a bottom turn, screams down the line, and ends it with an off-the-lip.

B) Via takes a late drop, does a sweeping bottom turn, heads up the middle of the wave, shoots down the wave, clears a closeout section, and does an off-the-lip.

C) Art paddles into a wave but gets pitched over the falls in a wipeout. He is underwater and struggles to the surface. At the surface, he gets a breathe of air, and regains his composure. He watches Via, in the FOREGROUND, drop in on the next wave and shred it. The huge wave that Via is surfing is approaching Art. Art takes a few breaths and dives underwater for the bottom. The white turbulence rushes over him, it goes dark for a split second, then light again, Art starts swimming for the surface, he comes up and takes a deep breath of air. Art watches Via further down the wave surfing and kicking out. SWITCH TO: Via sees Art in the FOREGROUND retrieving his board, getting on it, and paddling back out to the lineup.

D) Art redeems himself by taking off on another wave and surfing it flawlessly.

E) Via catches a wave and destroys it.

F) Art and Via are paddling back out to the lineup.

G) 2 surfers from the cliff vantage point watch Art catch a wave and surf it to perfection.

H) Art and Via paddle to the shoreline together.

EXT. BLUFF - DAY

Art and Via are sitting on a bluff full of tropical greenery. The bluff overlooks the bay. As they watch the waves roll in, Art is playing with a gecko that is nearby. Via, with a tranquil look, takes all the scenery in. She turns to Art.

                    VIA
It's good to see that some things never
change.

                    ART
                    What's that?

The gecko scurries up Art's arm and then back down again.

                    VIA
Oh, just that I can always count on you to
get me out of the rat race and back to
what surfing's all about.

Art looks up at Via.

                    ART
What surfing's all about? You're the
World Champ. You've done what every
surfer can only dream of.

                    VIA
I'd trade places with you any day.
Nobody owns you, you're free to surf
wherever and whenever you want. You
and the waves are one... in love with each
other.

Me... I'm a slave to surfing.

                    ART
How can you say that. You wouldn't
have gotten where you are today, if you
didn't love surfing.

      VIA

There was a time that may have been the true, but now my life is no more than an itinerary...

      ART

What do you mean by that?

      VIA

Well, tomorrow, I fly to Minnesota of all places! To do a promotional event at The Mall of America...

      ART

So What! Look at what you've accomplished! Your surfing has influenced and inspired thousands of girls around the globe. You have single handedly changed the face of surfing forever.   It's no longer a sport of kings. It's now a sport of kings and queens. Those girls look up to you! You're a role model for surfing. An inspiration to us all.

Via longingly looks out to the ocean, watches a wave peel off the reef, and then looks at Art.

      VIA

 I was wrong when I said soul surfing was
  dead...

Art gives Via a forgiving glance.

> ART
> We were both wrong. I should have
> taken your dreams seriously. Instead, I
> was holding you back. I wanted us to
> stay 16 and be friends forever.
>
> You were right, when you said, "We
> aren't kids anymore". And now that I'm
> older, I feel like life is a never-ending
> battle that is constantly dragging me
> away from the waves...

> VIA
> I know exactly what you mean. Life is
> pulling me away from the waves too,
> when...

> ART & VIA
> (Speaking the exact same words
> at the exact same time)
> All I want to do is surf...

Art and Via look at each other as if their 2 individual universes have just collided and become 1. Whatever differences they have had in the past, instantly vaporized. The bond that has been broken for all of these years, has been put back together. Art and Via have become the closest of friends once again.

Art turns away from Via for a moment, and fiddles with his ear. He turns back around. The gecko has clasped its mouth on Art's earlobe, and hangs there like an earring. Art looks at Via.

> ART
> Come on, let's get outta' here.

Via looks at Art and starts laughing. They get up and start walking down the trail with their BACKS FACING THE CAMERA. The gecko is still hanging off of Art's earlobe wiggling. Via looks at Art and the gecko clasping to his earlobe, and laughs.

VIA

You're such a kook.

They both start laughing as they walk away.

DISSOLVE TO:

BAJAN
SURFBOARDS

THE KEY

EXT. BACKYARD - DAY

Art is doing some ding repair on one of his surfboards in the backyard. There is a small patch of green grass that is surrounded by dense foliage such as banana plants, and guava bushes. There are also plants that have leaves which are the size and shape of elephant ears. Birds are chirping and a cat is cruising around the yard. Art with a look of concentration is working on his surfboard when all of a sudden, the phone rings. Art quits what he is doing and walks in the house to pick up the phone.

INT. LIVING ROOM - DAY

                    ART
          Hello...

              JOE (V.O. PHONE)
          Hey Art, it's Joe. Wuz D Word!

                    ART
          Hey! Howzit bruddah... Good to hear
          from you again. The summer tourist
          season's about over. When are you
          gonna come visit? It's been 7 years since
          I lcft.

              JOE (V.O. PHONE)
          Well, it could be pretty soon... I've
          decided to retire.

                    ART
          Retire? But you're the backbone of the
          surf community... You can't retire!

                    JOE (V.O. PHONE)
That's where you step in. You're the only
person who can keep the legacy of Bajan
Surfboards intact... Do you remember
that key I gave you a few years back?

                    ART
Yeah.

                    JOE (V.O. PHONE)
That's the key to Bajan Surfboards... I
want you to take over where I left off.

                    ART
What... Really???? But why me?

                    JOE (V.O. PHONE)
Ever since you were a small kid, I knew
that one day, I would hand over Bajan
Surfboards to you. Because you and I are
exactly the same... We're just a
generation apart. A new era of surfing is
upon us and it needs a younger person to
usher it in appropriately... You're that
person.

                    ART
          (confused & emotional)
I'm honored that you hold me in such
high regard... This is so much to take in.
So many things are rushing through my
head right now. I've got to think on this.

JOE (V.O. PHONE)
Take your time. You've always wanted
to own a surf shop... The new generation
needs someone they can look up too.
There's no one better than you!... This is
your chance...

FADE AWAY to Art talking on the phone.

DISSOLVE TO:

EXT. CLIFF POINT - DAY

Aiko is sitting on the cliff sanding the fins of another surfboard. Art walks
up to her.

ART
Nice day out here.

Art sits down next to Aiko and looks out to the ocean. Aiko quits sanding
for a moment and looks to the horizon.

AIKO
Yeah, it sure is.

Aiko pauses for a second and starts to sand again. Art picks up a blade of
grass and sticks it in his mouth. He picks a few more blades of grass and
starts silently ripping them into pieces as he looks out to the horizon. Aiko
notices a bit of uneasiness in Art's mannerisms.

AIKO
What's the matter? You haven't been
yourself lately.

ART
Oh, it's just that I got this phone call the
other day and I'm really confused.

>   AIKO
> Confused about what?

>   ART
> Remember Joe, the person I always talk
> about.

>   AIKO
> Yeah.

>   ART
> He wants me to take over the surf shop,
> and I've got mixed emotions about the
> whole thing. It's taken me years to be
> finally accepted on the island. People
> have just now quit asking me the
> question, "so Art when are you leaving?"
> I feel like if I just get up and move now,
> I've betrayed everyone here. Plus, I
> really love the island. This place is
> beautiful and the waves are insane. On
> the other hand, the primary reason I came
> here was to find my limitations in the
> water. I've felt like I have accomplished
> that goal. I'm not saying I mastered big
> wave surfing, no one can master it, but I
> have found my limitations. Maybe it's
> time to move on, and give something
> back to surfing. Move to a place where I
> can have a positive impact on younger
> surfers...

Art picks up more blades of grass. He unconsciously begins tearing them
as he looks out to the ocean.

                    ART
          Having my own surf shop puts me closer
          to the edge of leaving and starting a new
          chapter in life... I don't know. What do
          you think I should do?

                    AIKO
          All I can say is the choice has to come
          from within. But whatever outcome,
          make it a choice you'll never regret...
          Because the decisions you've made in the
          past, can never be reversed...

                    ART
          If I decide to leave, I don't want people
          here to think I'm a quitter... Especially
          you! I don't want to let you down.

                    AIKO
          You're the last person I would think of as
          a quitter.

Aiko looks at Art and smiles, then shifts her attention back to sanding the
fins on the surfboard.

                                                  CUT TO:

INT. ART'S BEDROOM - DAY

Leaning on the top of Art's dresser is the wax figurine that Art and Via
made as kids, the miniature wave house, and the colored sketch Ledge
gave him of all his friends back home. He picks up the sketch, looks at it,
and smiles.

                                                  DISSOLVE TO:

BAJAN
SURFBOARDS
OPEN

HOMECOMING

EXT. DILAPIDATED SHED - DAY

Art walks up to a dilapidated shed that has vines and unkept bushes growing all around it. He rips away some of the vines and brush to open the door to the shed.

INT. DILAPIDATED SHED - DAY

Art enters the shed. There are about 10 dusty surfboards stacked vertically against each other in bookend fashion. He starts feeling the outside rails of the surfboards and is in quiet reflection. His hand touches a surfboard with a light blue rail. He slowly pulls the surfboard out and wipes the dust off the board, revealing that this is his first surfboard he bought back when he was 10 years old. It's the light blue, single fin surfboard, with the large airbrushed wave on the deck. Art pauses, as he fondly thinks about his childhood memories.

EXT. BEACH - DAY

Art is standing on the sand dunes. Under his arm is the light blue single fin surfboard with the wave airbrushed on the deck. He stands there looking at the waves breaking. In the FOREGROUND, is the picnic table with a new generation of grommets hanging out. The grommets ages range from 10-12 years old. Art is reflecting on all the memories of the place where he grew up surfing. He looks around, smiles, and heads to the water. As Art walks past the picnic table, one of the younger grommets starts to crack on him.

                    GROMMET #4
            Where did this guy come from? The
            stone ages?

The group of grommets laugh.

                    GROMMET #4
            That single fin is the kind of board my
            great grandfather used to ride.

The grommets laugh again, Art turns around and makes eye contact with
the grommet who was making the wisecracks. Art smiles at him, turns
back around, and heads for the water.

EXT. LINEUP - DAY

A head high swell approaches. Art spins around and takes off. He trims
down the line with all the mastery and style of surfing a single fin. He
does a roller coaster up and down the face then shifts his feet to the center
of the board. At which time the wave jacks up and pitches out. Art tucks
into the barrel and gets tubed. He pops out of the tube, kicks out of the
wave, and paddles back out.

Art is sitting at the lineup taking in the scenery. Via paddles up next to
him and sits on her board.

                    VIA
            Hey Art! Long time, no see!

                    ART
            I never thought I'd see you here.

                    VIA
            We've got a 3-week gap between
            contests, and I thought I'd come visit the
            old stomping grounds.

                    ART
How's the tour going?

                    VIA
It's going great. The new guard is giving
me some stiff competition, but I'm still
hanging tough...

Via at peace with herself smiles at Art.

                    VIA
But I think my days of being a
professional surfer are slowly coming to
an end...

                    ART
You've had a great run... I'm so proud of
you. We are all proud of you.

Art hugs Via while sitting on the surfboard. Via does the same thing.

                    VIA
What are you doing on that old single
fin?

                    ART
This was my first surfboard. It needed
dusting. So, I thought I'd take it out for a
spin.

                    VIA
I remember that board! I wish I still had
my first board. It was an old beat up, 6-
foot G&S, triple stringer single fin.

                    ART
That's right! "The yellow banana".

Art and Via chuckle while reminiscing about their surfboards.

> VIA
>
> Joe told me the news about Bajan
> Surfboards. It can't be in better hands.

> ART
> (jokingly)
> Thanks. If you ever need to sponge a
> coupla' bars of wax, you know where to
> go.

Art sees a wave approaching, spins around, and catches the wave. He drops in and looks back at Via and hoots. Via laughs, smiles, and catches the next wave.

> DISSOLVE TO:

EXT. BAJAN SURFBOARDS - DAY

Art has the light blue surfboard under his arm along with a large wrinkled paper bag. He unlocks the front door of Bajan Surf Shop. He walks in and heads to the back of the store where all the surfboards are located. Above the office door is a shiny new surfboard hanging on the wall. He takes down the shiny surfboard and replaces it with his old light blue surfboard with the airbrushed wave on the deck. He takes the objects out of the paper bag which is the colored sketch Ledge gave him, the wax figurine, the wave house, and a picture of Aiko sitting on the cliff sanding a fin on a surfboard. He hangs the sketch and picture next to the old newspaper clippings of Joe when he was the surf champion of Barbados and places the wax figurine and wave house on the shelf next to the pictures. He takes a few steps back and looks at the wall. Art walks to the front of the store to the door. He pauses for a moment, turns around, looks at the surf shop, turns back around to the door, and flips the sign from CLOSED to OPEN. As Art walks away from the door, he notices some people entering. It's Joe, Via, Ledge, Devo, and Tuna.

Everyone has large smiles on their faces, they all look at each other, and come together in a joyous group hug.

DISSOLVE TO:

10 YEARS LATER

EXT. BEACH - MORNING (10 YEARS LATER)

7-YEAR-OLD TWINS, one boy and one girl, are near the shoreline. They are playing and building a sand castle. The camera PANS OUT to reveal 3 sets of people in the shot. 1) There is a person with a surfboard coming out of the ocean, 2) The twins building their sand castle, 3) The back of a beach chair with a person sitting in it next to the twins. The person sitting in the beach chair cannot be determined from this camera angle. All you see is the back of a head and a straw hat.

The person coming out of the water with the surfboard is Art! He is older and has a beard. Art smiles and winks at the twins. He then turns his attention to the person in the beach chair.

                    ART
          It's your turn.

The person gets up out of the beach chair with her BACK TO THE CAMERA and picks up a surfboard. With the board under her arm, she walks over and kisses Art. Art walks over to the twins. A CLOSEUP of the twins who have stopped building their sandcastle, look up with awe at Art.

Art looks at the twins with love in his eyes and pauses. He looks out to the ocean's horizon and pauses. Art remembers that day on the beach when he was 10 years old building a sand castle and encountering The Surfer. The day that he knew he wanted to be a surfer. He looks at the twins.

                    ART
          Do you want to go surfing with Mom &
          Dad?

The twins' eyes light up with excitement and eager anticipation. Art smiles and looks at the mom holding the surfboard.

ART
What do you say?

The mom walks over to the twins. A CLOSEUP of the twins looking up at her with awe. The camera PANS OUT to reveal an older yet eloquent and refined Via! Via blissfully smiles at Art and the twins.

VIA
Let's go surfing.

CUT TO:

With their BACKS FACING THE CAMERA, Via, Art, and the twins are all holding hands walking into the water for their first surf session together as a family.

FADE OUT.

www.tbbsurf.com